P9-CKH-367

The Many Lives of
BENJAMIN FRANKLIN

(The Library Company of Philadelphia)

THE MANY LIVES OF Benjamin Franklin

Mary Pope Osborne

DIAL BOOKS FOR YOUNG READERS
NEW YORK

Published by Dial Books for Young Readers
A Division of Penguin Books USA Inc.
375 Hudson Street
New York, New York 10014

Designed by Nancy R. Leo
Printed in the U.S.A.
E
First Edition
1 3 5 7 9 10 8 6 4 2

Library of Congress Cataloging in Publication Data
Osborne, Mary Pope.
The many lives of Benjamin Franklin / by Mary Pope Osborne.
p. cm.
Summary: A biography of the founding father, from his boyhood in Boston through his apprenticeship in the publishing business to his accomplishments as a printer, scientist, inventor, and statesman.
ISBN 0-8037-0679-0. ISBN 0-8037-0680-4 (lib. bdg.)
1. Franklin, Benjamin, 1706–1790—Juvenile literature.
2. Statesmen—United States—Biography—Juvenile literature.
3. Printers—United States—Biography—Juvenile literature.
4. Inventors—United States—Biography—Juvenile literature.
5. Scientists—United States—Biography—Juvenile literature.
[1. Franklin, Benjamin, 1706–1790. 2. Statesmen.]
I. Title.
E302.6.F8078 1990 973.3'092'4—dc19 [B] [92] 88-38369 CIP AC

For Carl and M. D. Schnabel
and all their family

TABLE OF CONTENTS

(The Library Company of Philadelphia)

INTRODUCTION

OVER three hundred years ago, a silk dyer named Josiah Franklin decided to leave England, the land of his ancestors. Josiah longed to practice religion the way he wanted to, not the way the Church of England told him to. Some of his friends were traveling to an unusual new country where there was religious freedom, and he decided to go with them. So, in 1683, Josiah Franklin, his wife Ann, and three children packed their belongings and set sail for America.

At that time America was not yet a unified republic. The country was made up of thirteen separate colonies which were considered part of the British Empire. Even though all the colonies used English as their language, each was very different from the next. There was no single church and no one way of life. There were Boston Puritans, Philadelphia Quakers, western frontiersmen, Native American Indians, southern planters, Blacks from Africa, as well as people from Germany, Scotland, France, Iceland, Switzerland, and many other countries. The thirteen colonies hugged the eastern coast of America. Beyond them lay huge, untamed territories claimed by France and Spain.

When Josiah and his family landed in America, they settled in Boston, a busy seaport city in the colony of Massachusetts. Boston was inhabited by people called Puritans. The Puritans were members of a religious group that had come to America in the 1600s and settled in Virginia and on the coast of New England. As the Puritans shaped the government and the social life of Boston, they preached the value of hard work and education. They were also very strict about morals and religious matters.

Josiah soon learned that the serious-minded Puritans had little time for such frivolities as dyed silk. In order to support his quickly growing family, he changed his trade and became a soap maker and candle maker.

But not long after Josiah and his family were settled into their new life, tragedy struck. After Ann Franklin gave birth for the last time, both she and the child died. In those days, without modern medicine, women frequently died in childbirth, and one out of four infants died within a few days of birth. Children also died of many common diseases, such as smallpox, scarlet fever, and dysentery.

After Ann's death, Josiah was left with five children to care for. But within a year he found a new mother for them—Abiah Folger, a descendant of early New England settlers. Abiah was an unusually hearty woman. Though she and Josiah had ten more children, she was never sick a day until her death at the age of eighty-five.

In 1706, on a cold January morning, in a rented house on Milk Street, Josiah Franklin's last son was born. Josiah and Abiah named the boy Benjamin, after Josiah's favorite brother. Benjamin Franklin was a strong, healthy baby, and he soon was Josiah's favorite child. His father probably delighted in the fact that Benjamin was the youngest son of the youngest son for five generations—in other words, he was the youngest son of the youngest son of the youngest son of the youngest son of the youngest son. Perhaps this was a lucky omen, for one day this youngest son would grow up to be one of the most amazing persons who ever lived. Not only would he become one of the founders of the United States, but he would also become an important writer, an extraordinary diplomat, a fine scientist, and a great inventor.

The Many Lives of BENJAMIN FRANKLIN

He snatched the lightning from heaven,
and the scepter from kings.

A.R.J. TURGOT,
eighteenth-century French economist

A Boy in Boston

From a child I was fond of reading, and all the little money that came into my hands was ever laid out in books.
—*from* The Autobiography of Benjamin Franklin

AT THE TIME of Ben Franklin's birth, there were about a thousand houses in the city of Boston. Painted in bright colors, they were huddled together on narrow cobblestone streets. They had as few windows as possible to keep out the bitter winter winds. Although several of Josiah's children had already left home and four had died, a huge family still remained. Probably at least six children were still at home at the time of Ben's birth. The whole family lived together in four rooms and had only one fireplace for heat.

As a small child, Ben Franklin was bright and curious. One of his first memories was of an event that happened when he was seven. One day he was given

A reproduction of a painting of Franklin's birthplace in Boston. The house was destroyed by fire in 1810. (The Library Company of Philadelphia)

some money to spend, and, on his way to a shop, he met an older boy blowing a whistle. Ben thought the whistle was so wonderful that he bought it from the boy, giving him all his money. Then he joyfully carried the whistle home to show to his family. But his brothers and sisters teased him, saying that he had paid four times too much for the little whistle. His pride was so hurt that he never forgot the lesson. Years later he often wrote about the value of thrift, and used the whistle as an example of giving too much for the wrong thing. Once he wrote, "The great part of the miseries of mankind were brought upon them by the false estimates they had made of the value of things, and by their giving too much for the whistle."

As a boy, Ben tried to save time as well as money. Since he always grew impatient when his father said long blessings at mealtimes, one day he suggested that Josiah say a blessing over the family's whole supply of meat at one time. That way he wouldn't have to pray over every single meal.

Growing up in a seaport town surrounded by water, Ben enjoyed swimming in the ponds near Boston's salt marshes. He studied a little book on swimming, which taught him a number of bizarre water tricks, such as swimming with his hands completely still, or with both of his feet out of the water, or with his legs tied together. He worked on these and many more swimming feats until he became one of the best swimmers in Boston.

Ben also enjoyed building little boats and canoes—and experimenting with new water inventions. For instance, he invented a primitive pair of swimming flippers, and another time, he held onto the string of a kite and was pulled across a pond by the power of wind.

The title page illustration in an 1852 book, The Works of Benjamin Franklin, *shows Franklin as a boy being pulled through the water by a kite. (American Philosophical Society)*

Ben and his friends loved to fish for minnows in the salt marsh. But they grew tired of standing in the murky water, so one day they decided to build a small wharf to fish from. Earlier Ben had discovered a heap of stones intended for a new house. That night when the workmen left, he led the boys to the stones, and they carried them away and built their little wharf. The next day after the workmen found the missing stones, they told the boys' fathers about the theft. Ben tried to convince Josiah of the usefulness of his deed. But Josiah convinced him "that nothing was useful which was not honest."

Josiah was a strong influence on his son. Ben later wrote in his autobiography that his father was very strong and was very handy with tools. He could also draw well and was skilled in music and had a clear and pleasing voice. Ben said that at the end of the day, Josiah often played his violin and sang hymns.

But Ben thought Josiah's greatest skill was in advising others. Many people came to consult Josiah Franklin about town and church affairs. Ben remembered that his father frequently invited learned guests to dinner so that his children could benefit from the conversations that took place among the grownups. These discussions were so fascinating to Ben that he hardly noticed his food at all.

Josiah Franklin was very concerned about the future of his children in the New World. In those days, many young people left home to seek their fortune elsewhere, and seldom returned. Sons became sailors or explorers, and daughters headed into the wilderness to marry settlers. Josiah was heartbroken when his oldest son ran off to sea, so he tried to make sure that the rest of his sons acquired a trade on land. In those days, having a trade meant knowing how to do something very useful, such as making candles, or working as a blacksmith, or printing books and newspapers. Since modern machinery had not yet been invented and there were no large factories, everything had to be done by hand. So if a man knew how to do something very well, he could always find work. Josiah believed that having a trade would also allow his sons to save money and acquire property—and thus give them a firm foothold in the New World.

But since his youngest son was so bright and loved to read so much, Josiah decided that Ben shouldn't be a tradesman—he should become the family's one clergyman instead. Since clergymen had to be very well educated, it would be necessary to send Ben to a good school. When he was eight, his father sent him to Boston Grammar School to begin his education. But after only one year Josiah changed his mind. He decided that training Ben to be a clergyman was too expensive. Besides, he reasoned, once a man became a minister, he was very poorly paid.

Josiah took Ben out of the Boston Grammar School

and sent him to a more ordinary school. There he did well in writing, but when he failed in arithmetic, he was sent back home. This marked the end of Ben Franklin's formal education—and he was not yet ten years old.

After he left school, Ben began assisting in his father's soap and candle shop. He cut wicks for candles, poured hot wax into molds, attended to the

Eighteenth-century candle-making shop. (Dover Books)

shop, and ran errands. But after two years, he began to dislike the work. And soon he was dreaming about running away and becoming a sailor. After all, he was a strong swimmer and was quite skilled with boats. But since his father greatly feared losing Ben to the sea, he took time off from his candle making and walked with Ben around Boston so that Ben could observe the different trades and choose the one he liked best.

Ben loved watching the bricklayers, brass workers, printers, leather workers, carpenters, and other tradesmen. Later in life he said that his love for different tools began at this time. But now he faced a hard decision that would affect the rest of his life. What tools did he love the most? Which did he want to learn how to use?

Ben could not remember a time when he didn't know how to read. He enjoyed a book called *Pilgrim's Progress*, about the journey of a good Puritan. Two other early favorites were *Plutarch's Lives*, about the lives of early heroes, and *Essays to Do Good*, by a famous Puritan clergyman, Cotton Mather. Ben loved reading so much that he asked his father if he could learn to be a printer.

Josiah already had one son who was a printer. Twenty-one-year-old James Franklin had just returned from England with a printing press and was about to set up his own shop in Boston. Josiah had wanted each of his sons to have a different profession. But after thinking it over, he decided it was all right to have two sons as printers, so he allowed Ben to become James's apprentice.

When he was only twelve years old, Benjamin

Franklin signed a contract promising that until he was twenty-one, he would work for his brother James and learn the printer's trade. It was a major commitment for a boy so young.

Apprentice

Perhaps I was too saucy and provoking.
—*from* The Autobiography of
Benjamin Franklin

THE LIFE of an apprentice in the 1700s might not seem very fair to us today. Twelve-year-old Ben Franklin promised his brother James that he would work without pay until he was twenty-one years old. He gave his word that while he was an apprentice, he would not get married, not play cards, not drink alcohol, and not go to plays. Even though James was only nine years older than he, Ben had to promise to obey him at all times.

In exchange for these promises, Ben would be given food, clothing, and a room. And he would get one good suit when he turned twenty-one. But most important of all, in exchange for hard discipline and a few years of servitude, he would learn a craft that would serve him all of his life, a craft that would bring him a great deal of respect and satisfaction. Printing was a craft that suited Ben better than candle making.

The atmosphere in James's tiny, ink-smelling shop must have been exciting, for in early America a printing office was the center for news and opinions. Being a printer was physically demanding as well, for the wooden press that James had brought from England was run by hand.

For three hundred years the same type of printing

Two printing presses. The one on the left is being inked; the one on the right is printing a sheet. (Dover Books)

press had been in use. It was a handpress invented by a man named Gutenberg in the 1400s. Before Gutenberg's invention, all books had to be written by hand—so there could never be more than a few copies of any book. The printing press, however, provided a way to apply type to a piece of paper and make many copies of the same page in a short period of time. Usually two people worked at the press. First one put little letters into a case called a composing stick. Then he put ink on the letters. The

The composing room of an eighteenth-century print shop. The typesetters in the middle and on the left are placing letters on the composing stick. The printer on the right is preparing a page of type. Printed pages are hanging to dry from rods near the ceiling. (Dover Books)

other worker pulled down a bar that brought the inky-wet composing stick onto a sheet of white paper. It took two pulls to get the paper completely printed. Then after the wet letters were printed onto the paper, the paper was hung over wooden rods to dry. In order to get three hundred copies of a pamphlet or newspaper, all these actions had to be repeated three hundred times! It wasn't until many years later that machines rapidly turned out sheets of printed matter.

As far as the record shows, from the age of twelve to sixteen, Ben Franklin had no time for sports or for socializing with boys and girls his own age. Wearing his white shirt and leather apron, he seemed to have spent nearly all his time working in the printing office. The only thing he did when he wasn't working was read and study. Booksellers' apprentices lent him their masters' books to read overnight. Ben not only read the greater part of the night, but he also read early in the mornings, after work, and on Sundays. He became a freethinker, which meant he no longer went to church. And he became a vegetarian because he didn't want to eat the flesh of slaughtered animals.

After Ben became a vegetarian, he struck a deal with his brother James. He volunteered to buy his own food for half of the money James was paying a boardinghouse to feed him. Then when James and other workers went to eat, Ben stayed behind and ate a biscuit or a slice of bread or just some raisins. While he ate his meager food, he read books and studied. He studied navigation, philosophy, and English grammar. He also taught himself how to do arithmetic—the very subject he had failed years earlier. By eating so simply, Ben only spent half of the money James gave him (which was only one fourth of the amount that had been paid to the boarding-house). With his savings Ben bought more books.

Franklin as a young printer's apprentice, reading borrowed books by candlelight. (American Philosophical Society)

The more he read, the more he wanted to be a writer himself. So one day he wrote a ballad about Blackbeard, the pirate who had been killed off the coast of North Carolina in 1717. He also wrote a ballad called "The Lighthouse Tragedy," about a family that drowned at sea. He printed the ballads onto white sheets, then sold them in the streets. In those days, original ballads were very popular, and some men were able to sell enough to make their living at it. But Ben's father made fun of his verses and told Ben that verse writers were "generally beggars." So even though his pieces had been quite successful, Ben followed his father's advice and gave up ballad writing.

But Ben still wanted to be a writer. Since he could not go to school to learn how to write well, he figured out a way to teach himself. First, he collected copies of an excellent newspaper called the *Spectator*. This daily paper, published in England in 1711 and 1712, had greatly influenced many writers with its simple and elegant style. Ben jotted down the ideas in the *Spectator*'s articles and then put them away. After a few days he wrote the ideas in his own words. He then compared his sentences to the *Spectator*'s sentences. He did this again and again, until he thought he had even improved upon the original articles.

Ben began to use his new writing skills to compose secret letters to his brother's paper. At that time,

James was publishing a newspaper called the *New England Courant*. Many people had tried to discourage him from starting the *Courant*. They said the country didn't need another paper. But James and his staff thought the other newspapers in Boston were dull and dreary. So they took it upon themselves to criticize everything in town, including the leading Puritan clergymen and city officials.

Ben, eager to join the battle, wrote many funny opinions about things going on in the Boston world. He was afraid that James wouldn't print anything he wrote, so he signed his articles with a fake name: Mrs. Silence Dogood. Then he slipped them under the printing-house door.

The *Courant* writers loved the mysterious writings of Mrs. Dogood and immediately printed them. James and his friends speculated about which leading citizen was pretending to be the busybody widow. She had an opinion on everything from hoopskirts to town drunkards. Mrs. Dogood also supported the idea of educating women. At that time, since the Puritans opposed women's rights, most Boston women were not even taught to read and write. Ben Franklin, however, was on the side of women. In his early teens, he wrote letters to a friend, arguing in favor of educating women. All his life he seemed to have a special closeness with women, as he had many women friends.

At sixteen, Ben was an odd-looking boy. He was thickset with a very large head. He had a homely, friendly face, and was nearly six feet—which was unusually tall for that time. He must have attracted a lot of attention as he worked away in the printing shop, for not only was he exceptionally strong and

Bronze bas-relief on the base of Greenough's statue of Franklin in front of City Hall in Boston, showing Franklin as an apprentice printer. (American Philosophical Society)

hearty, but he also had a magnetic personality and an amazing intelligence—perhaps even the best mind in the city of Boston.

Ben's brother, James, seemed to have been jealous of him. When Ben finally confessed that he was Mrs. Silence Dogood, James was not pleased. He angrily accused Ben of becoming vain because of all the praise he must have heard about himself. In those days, it was not at all uncommon for a master to discipline an apprentice by striking him. James often struck Ben when he was angry at him. Ben confesses in his autobiography that perhaps he was too "saucy and provoking," but he also says that he greatly resented the blows he got from James. Though he never comes right out and says that he disliked James, he says that his lifelong dislike for tyrannical power began when his brother abused him.

Escape from Boston

. . . so I stopt at a poor inn where I staid all night, beginning now to wish that I had never left home.

—*from* The Autobiography of Benjamin Franklin

SOON JAMES FRANKLIN faced worse problems than being jealous of his brother Ben. In those days, before America was a united republic, there was no constitution that guaranteed freedom of the press as there is today. If local officials did not like what someone wrote, they could put that person in jail. Since many of the *Courant* articles aroused the anger of the leading clergy and members of the city government of Boston, James was headed for trouble.

Cotton Mather, the famous Puritan clergyman, was especially offended. Mather, who had been involved years before in the Salem witch trials, accused James and his writers of worshiping the devil. He called them the Hell Fire Club. The city's officials were also eager to punish the *Courant* for criticizing them. So when James mocked the officials for not trying hard enough to capture pirates off the coast, they locked him in jail for a month.

James begged to be let out of prison, but the officials would only let him go if he promised to be the publisher of the *Courant* no longer. James agreed, and, in public, he turned the title of publisher over to his younger brother, Ben. But secretly he signed a contract with Ben that said he was still Ben's master and Ben was still his apprentice.

Ben, however, took advantage of James's public act and refused to work for him anymore. He had outgrown his role as apprentice. He found the work tedious and demeaning. At seventeen, he had already proved himself as a ballad writer, a newspaper columnist, a humorist, a political thinker, a printer, and a publisher. It was time to move on.

Ben's father and James did not see it Ben's way, however. They thought Ben had cheated James out of four years of free labor. James was so angry that he went to all the other printers in Boston and urged them not to hire his brother. The printers agreed to honor James's request, for in those days, the contract between a master and an apprentice was almost a sacred agreement. Newspapers even advertised rewards for the capture of runaway apprentices.

So before he was eighteen years old, Ben Franklin decided to escape from Boston. He seemed to have

[No 26

THE New-England Courant.

From MONDAY December 11. to MONDAY December 18. 1721.

To the Author of the New-England Courant

SIR,

Dec. 8. 1721.

SINCE in your last *Courant* you was pleased to say, *That both Anti-Inoculators and Inoculators should be welcome to speak their Minds in your Paper*, I send the following Reasons against inoculating the Small Pox, which I hope in pursuance of your Promise, you will insert in your next, if you have Room.

The First Reason then is, That this Operation being perform'd upon none but such as are in perfect Health, and who, for any thing the Doctor or Patients know, may be such who may never have that Distemper in their Lives, or if they have, not to that Degree as to make it mortal to them: and then surely it must be needless to the last Degree, for any Man to have himself made sick in order to prevent that which for any thing he knows, he is in no Danger of.

But in the Second Place, much more so, when the Persons that are for that Operation, cannot answer this Small Question to the Satisfaction of any rational Creature, viz. *Whether this Operation is Infallible, so that hitherto there is not any Body has perished, that has had the Small Pox produced by it.* I say, this is a Point the World will find them for ever tender upon: And altho' they would fain insinuate that it is infallible, yet they will never give you a direct Answer, but will put you off with this, *That there is nothing infallible in Physick; for that they have known Persons dye by a Vomit, and others by Bleeding*, &c. But allowing what they say to be true, for once; these Gentlemen never distinguish betwixt making a *well Man sick*, and endeavouring to make a *sick Man well*; for certainly, there is not any thing will defend any Man's bringing a Sickness on himself, unless he is sure that he cannot die of that Illness he does so bring upon him; for we are obliged to preserve the Health we have, as much as we are obliged to preserve our Lives: Whereas on the other Hand, in giving of *Vomits*, &c. it is never done by wise Physicians, but to Persons who have *really lost their Healths*, and of Course it is allowable to run a little Risque to recover that Health which it has pleased God to take from him. But let these Gentlemen talk as they will about such things, I dare say that every reasonable Man will think it very ridiculous, to compare Inoculating the Small Pox to *Bleeding* or *Vomiting*, &c. when the one is done to none but such as are in perfect Health, and the other to Persons that are sick. Besides, I have seen Physick practised by some of the ablest Physicians that ever the World saw, and have been practising of it my self this twenty Years past. But I must say, I never saw any Man die by *Bleeding* or *Blistering*, or by *Vomiting* or *Purging*, provided they were given in proper Doses. But if ignorant People, who neither understand Physick nor the Doses of Medicines, will be doing what they should not do, no Wonder if we see Instances of these innocent Things proving Mortal: But then the Fault is to be put to the Account of the *Persons who gave the things ignorantly*, and not to the *things themselves*. But it is quite otherwise with *Inoculation*; for there is not any Body that I know that can tell the Dose of that Juice so as to make it infallible. But he must be a very poor & heedless Physician indeed, that cannot prevent the aforesaid *Bleeding*, &c. from being hurtful to any Body.

And the third Reason is, that if they should say, *Inoculating the Small Pox is an infallible way to preserve Life.* I say, if they should say so, yet it is false in Fact; For Dr. *Emanuel Timonius* in his Letter to the Royal Society, owns, that he saw Two die that were Inoculated; but at the same Time would fain insinuate, that they died of some other Distemper, which is the very Error his Disciples on this side the Great *Atlantick* fall into; for when they are ask'd, *If it be Infallible, how came Mrs. D——l and several others to die of it?* They answer, She and they did not die of the *Small Pox*, but of some *other Distemper*, or else had received the Infection the Common Way first; which is certainly very ridiculous if one considers the following things.

Every Body knows that it's the Nature of *Hellebore* to purge; and of Course too great a Dose of it taken will kill any Man: And for any Body to say, that had given an excessive Dose of it to a Patient, and that Patient had purged to Death by it; I say, to say that that that Patient died of *some other Distemper*, would certainly be very ridiculous; and so is it every whit as ridiculous to say, that a Person that is in perfect Health, and is inoculated, and has the Effects of that Operation the same way as others have that have taken the utmost Precaution, *viz.* the *same Fever*, the *same Pustules*, only the Fever *more violent*, and a *greater Quantity* of Pustules, and at last *Death*. I say, It would be very ridiculous for any to say, that such Persons did not dy of the *Inoculated Small Pox*; when, as I said before, they had the Small Pox after that Operation, and were in perfect Health before it was performed upon them; which is the very Case of Mrs. *D——l*, and the rest of them that have dyed by it, so far as I can learn. As to Mrs. *D——l*, this I know, that they boasted much of having made such a Convert, and owned publickly that she had got the Small Pox by Inoculation. But when it pleased God to shew them that she must depart this Life, notwithstanding their Infallible Remedy; *Oh!* then they turn their Tones, and say truly, she dyed of *Hysterick*; which by the way, are the worst Fits they could have pitch'd upon; for of all Fits they prove the seldomest Mortal: And it it is as certain as the Sun shines at Noon in a clear Day, that she died of the Small Pox, which she received by Inoculation; and Mr. *B——n* himself must have thought so too, otherwise he was a very silly Man to inoculate her, when he had reason to suspect she had received the Infection the Common Way first, which probably might spoil the Reputation of his infallible Remedy.

Mr

A title page of the New England Courant *during the time that Ben was an apprentice to his brother James. (Massachusetts Historical Society)* no other choice: His family was angry with him. He could not get a job at any other printing house in town. And through his political writings, he'd made many enemies.

Since Ben feared that his father might try to prevent him from leaving Boston, he secretly sold his precious books. Then he slipped away on a ship heading down the coast to New York, the nearest city where he might find employment as a printer.

After three days of calm sailing, Ben's ship docked near New York. There he watched the other passengers fry a catch of codfish. He had loved eating fish when he was younger, but he would no longer eat them because of his vegetarian diet. The fish smelled so good, however, he could hardly bear it. Then with great relief, he soon discovered that when the fish were cut open, small fish were inside their stomachs. "If you eat one another, I don't see why we mayn't eat you," Ben said to the fish. And he dined happily. Thereafter, he only returned to his vegetarian diet now and then.

In New York, Franklin couldn't find a job as a printer. But someone suggested that he search for work in Philadelphia, a city one hundred miles south of New York. So he set out across the bay in a boat headed for Perth Amboy, New Jersey. From there he would walk fifty miles to the town of Burlington, New Jersey, and then catch a boat and sail down the Delaware River to Philadelphia. As his rickety ship crossed the bay, a terrible squall blew the ship off course and tore the sails to pieces. A drunken Dutchman fell into the water, but Ben saved him by grabbing him by the hair and drawing him up out of the sea.

When the ship finally reached Perth Amboy, Ben was very ill. He had been in the tossing boat for thirty hours without food or drink. He must have felt very alone as he shivered with a high fever. But practical as ever, he remembered reading that cold water was good for a fever, so he drank glass after glass of water. Whether this strange remedy was the cure or not, he was much better by morning.

The next day, barely recovered from illness, Ben began walking the fifty miles from Perth Amboy, across the colony of New Jersey, to Burlington. As he walked, still weak from his fever, another storm hit, and he was drenched with rain. When he finally found an inn, people suspected he might be a runaway servant. By now he was beginning to wish he had never left home.

When Ben finally arrived at Burlington, he discovered that all the boats had set sail, and another one would not be leaving for three more days. Later, however, as he walked along the river, several people came by in a boat. When he asked if he could ride with them, they took him in.

Since there was no wind, Ben and his companions had to row in the dark. At midnight they discovered they were lost, so they went ashore and made a fire with fence rails as they waited through the cold October night. As daylight approached, the group continued on their way, until they landed at Market Street wharf on a quiet Sunday morning.

Hungry, dirty, and exhausted, Ben Franklin had finally arrived in Philadelphia.

Journeyman and Printer

But what shall we think of a governor's playing such pitiful tricks, and imposing so grossly on a poor ignorant boy!
—*from* The Autobiography of Benjamin Franklin

FIFTY YEARS before Ben Franklin's arrival, Philadelphia, Pennsylvania, was wild woods where only Indians lived. But in 1682, a religious group called the Quakers landed in the wilderness after a grueling voyage from England. The Quaker leader, William Penn, made friends with the Indians whose ancestors had lived in that area for thousands of years. Then he set about building his little wilderness colony which was called the "City of Brotherly Love."

By the time of Ben's arrival in 1723 Philadelphia had grown into a large commercial center. There were flour mills, steel furnaces, and paper mills on the Delaware River. The city had gone from being a Quaker haven to a thriving, bustling city with a population of ten thousand people. As Ben walked up Market Street, he passed shops owned by tailors, saddle makers, joiners, wig makers, innkeepers, and printers. Ben's autobiography describes his state that first morning:

> *I was dirty from my journey; my pockets were stuffed out with shirts and stockings, and I knew no soul nor where to look for lodging. I was fatigued with travelling, rowing, and want of rest. I was very hungry; and my whole stock of cash consisted of a Dutch dollar, and about a shilling in copper.*

When he went into a bakery, he was pleasantly surprised to discover that huge puffy rolls were quite cheap. He bought three of them—stuck two under

Peter Cooper's painting of the city of Philadelphia in 1724, soon after

an arm as he gobbled the third. Continuing on his way up the street, he passed the door of a young woman named Deborah Reed. As Deborah stared at the disheveled young man, she must have thought he looked quite ridiculous. Little did she realize that this grubby boy would someday be her husband.

Ben knew no one in Philadelphia, and he had no idea where to go or what to do. He was so tired that he finally decided to follow a group of Quakers into a meeting house, the place where they gathered to sit together in silent worship. Ben sat on one of the simple wooden benches in the plain room, and in the peaceful silence, he promptly fell asleep.

Just as Boston was dominated by the Puritans' somber way of life, Philadelphia was strongly influenced by its Quaker origins. Like the Puritans, the

Franklin had arrived. (The Library Company of Philadelphia)

Quakers valued thrift and hard work. But unlike the Puritans, the Quakers were quite friendly and relaxed. They were far more tolerant of an untidy stranger than the Boston Puritans would have been. As Ben slept in their midst, no one demanded that he leave. He was gently wakened at the end of the meeting.

Once Ben was back on the street, another Quaker not only gave him advice about which rooming house to stay in, but he took him there as well. Ben immediately went to bed and slept the rest of the day—without even bothering to change out of his dirty traveling clothes.

Bright and early on Monday morning he set out to look for a printing job. It wasn't long before he found one with a man named Keimer. Keimer welcomed Ben into his shabby little printing shop and made him a journeyman. He also helped Ben obtain lodgings at a nearby house—the home of Deborah Reed, the girl who had gaped at Ben on his first morning in Philadelphia.

Through Deborah and her mother, Ben met other young people his age. He never had trouble making friends or getting people to help him. Throughout his life his good humor and charm drew others to him like a magnet. Now he gathered around him a group of friends who loved reading as much as he did. These friends discussed books and wrote to each other on different topics.

Ben also became friends with one of the most powerful men in Philadelphia. One day Keimer, his employer, was shocked when the governor of Pennsylvania, William Keith, came into the shop, asking for Benjamin Franklin. Keimer was further astounded when the governor asked Ben to join him for a bottle of wine.

At a nearby tavern, the governor explained that he knew Ben's seafaring brother-in-law. And when Governor Keith had read a letter that Ben had written to his brother-in-law, he'd resolved to seek out the brilliant young letter-writer. Now that Keith had met Ben, he was even more impressed. He offered to help Ben set up his own printing house in Philadelphia, then help him become the official printer of the colony.

Ben was pleased with the governor's attentions. From then on, he had frequent meetings with him, keeping them a secret from Keimer. The governor promised Ben that he would help set him up in his own business as soon as Ben could get money from his father. Governor Keith gave Ben a letter to take to Josiah in Boston, explaining his offer.

Seven months after he'd run away from home, Ben returned to Boston, carrying the governor's letter. His family had not heard a word from him since he'd left, and they were overjoyed to see him.

His brother James was the only one not happy at his return. When Ben entered James's printing shop,

James looked him over, then sullenly turned away. The other workers, though, were impressed when Ben showed off his new suit, a pocketful of silver coins, and his new watch. He was obviously living in much better circumstances than when he'd been James's apprentice. James later told his mother that he would never forgive Ben for humiliating him in front of his fellow workers. He was mistaken, however, for years later the brothers were reconciled, and when James died in his thirties, he even asked Ben to raise his son Jemmy. Ben sent Jemmy to school in Boston, then taught him the art of the printing trade.

Though Josiah Franklin was happy to see Ben, he refused to give him money to start his own printing company. Josiah thought Governor Keith was foolish to want to set up a seventeen-year-old boy in business. He was pleased, however, that Ben had impressed such an important official. This time when Ben set sail from Boston, at least he had his father's blessing.

Governor Keith was not discouraged when Ben told him his father wouldn't give him money to start a shop. Keith suggested that Ben journey to London to purchase printing equipment. He said Ben would have no trouble purchasing the equipment if he took along letters of credit from himself, the governor of Pennsylvania.

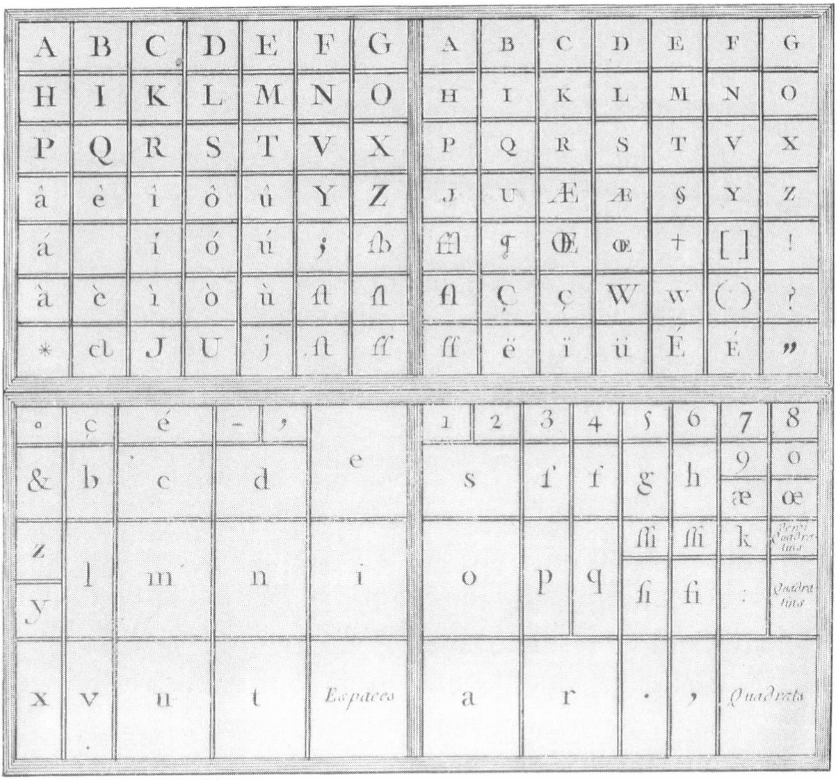

An eighteenth-century typecase, which holds the letters for the printing press. (Dover Books)

During this time Ben had grown quite fond of Deborah Reed, his landlady's daughter. Since Deborah felt the same way about Ben, they began to talk of marriage. But when Deborah's mother found out that Ben was soon leaving, she urged the two eighteen-year-olds to wait until he returned from London.

As Ben prepared to leave by ship, he called on Governor Keith, asking for his letters of credit. Keith's secretary told him the letters were not ready yet, but they would soon be delivered to the ship. On November 5, 1724, the day the ship sailed, Ben was very relieved when a friend of the governor's showed up at the last minute and handed a packet of letters to the captain. The captain, however, would not let anyone look at the letters until the ship had arrived in England.

On the stormy six-week voyage across the Atlantic, Ben became good friends with a Quaker merchant named Denham. Denham was a good and honest man who became like a second father to Ben. As the ship approached London on the day before Christmas, Ben looked among the mail for his letters from Governor Keith. He was horrified to discover that none of the letters bore his name. His worst fears had come true—he was about to land in London without money or a job!

When Ben sought the advice of his new friend Denham, Denham told him that Governor Keith had a habit of misleading people and that no one could depend upon him. Denham then advised Ben to learn as much as he could about the printing business in England and save his money so he could return home.

So, soon after his arrival, at eighteen years of age, Ben got a job at Samuel Palmer's Printing House, one of the most famous printing houses in the world. As usual, it wasn't long before he began to draw attention to himself. While he was working at his new job, he wrote a pamphlet on religion. The pamphlet expressed his freethinking ideas, which were quite different from the ideas of the church. Ben said that men were machines driven by nature, and that there was no right and no wrong. It was a scandalous piece that caused some of London's most scholarly men to take note of him because they shared the same thoughts. Later, however, Ben became ashamed of these views, and he destroyed most of the pamphlets.

> I grew convinc'd that *truth*, *sincerity*, and *integrity* in dealings between man and man were of the utmost importance. . . . Certain actions might not be bad *because* they were forbidden . . . yet probably these actions might be forbidden *because* they were bad for us, or commanded *because* they were beneficial to us, in their own natures.

Ben also gained attention for his amazing swimming abilities. In the Thames River he practiced the remarkable feats that he'd learned as a boy, prompting a nobleman to offer him a job teaching his children to swim. But Ben refused that job, for after eighteen months in London, he was ready to return to America. When his Quaker friend Denham offered him a job in his Philadelphia department store, he gladly accepted.

The voyage home was very rough and took almost three months. Shortly after he arrived in Philadelphia, Ben passed Governor Keith in the street. During the time he'd been away in London, Keith had been recalled from office as governor and was now a private citizen. Ben thought the man who'd betrayed him seemed ashamed, for Keith passed him without saying a word.

Ben himself felt ashamed for the way he had treated Deborah Reed. During his long absence he had written her only once, saying he would be gone for a long time. So, at the urging of her friends, Deborah had gone ahead and married another man, but when her husband turned out to be quite cruel, she'd left him. Since divorce was rare and was considered disgraceful in those days, she was now in a terrible state—neither married nor unmarried.

If life was difficult for Deborah at this time, it also became difficult for Ben. For a while he lived and worked happily with his kind friend Denham. But then he became ill with a severe cough and fever. At the same time, Denham began to suffer from an unknown ailment, and after a long illness, died. Not only did Ben lose a man he loved and respected, but he lost his new job as well. According to his autobiography, he was "once more to the wide world."

After searching for a new job, Ben found work with Keimer, the printer he'd worked for before his trip to London. Keimer was very short-tempered, and soon the two began to have terrible quarrels. Finally Ben broke from Keimer and set up his own printing shop with a partner. When he was twenty-four, he became sole owner of the shop and began publishing a newspaper called *The Pennsylvania Gazette*.

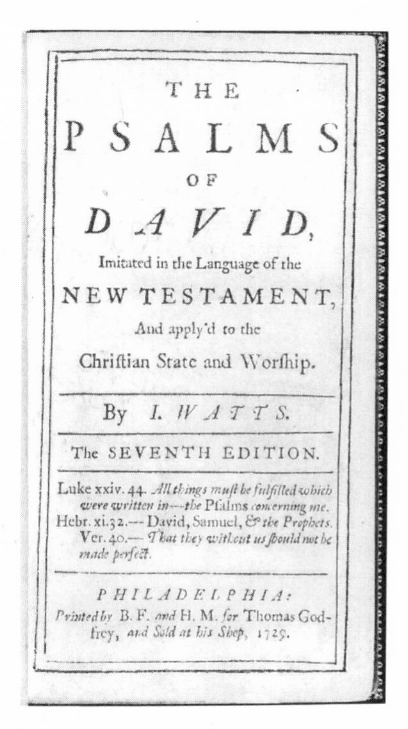
THE
PSALMS
OF
DAVID,
Imitated in the Language of the
NEW TESTAMENT,
And apply'd to the
Chriſtian State and Worſhip.

By *I. WATTS.*

The SEVENTH EDITION.

Luke xxiv. 44. *All things muſt be fulfilled which were written in*---*the* Pſalms *concerning me.*
Hebr. xi.32.--- David, Samuel, *& the Prophets.*
Ver. 40.--- *That they without us ſhould not be made perfect.*

PHILADELPHIA:
Printed by B. F. *and* H. M. *for* Thomas Godfrey, *and Sold at his Shop*, 1729.

An edition of the Psalms of David, printed by Franklin in his first independent shop in 1729. (The Library Company of Philadelphia)

That same year Ben also became the husband of Deborah Reed. Ben and Deborah were not married in a church, however, because they were afraid to get legally married. There had been rumors that Deborah's cruel first husband was dead, but there was no proof of his death. If he turned up suddenly, Ben and Deborah could be accused of bigamy, whipped with thirty-nine lashes, and imprisoned for life. For this reason they did not have a formal wedding ceremony, but once they began living together, everyone viewed them as husband and wife.

Deborah Franklin was a strong and loving woman. She raised William, Ben's small son by another woman—a mystery woman whom history has never identified. It seems that Ben brought William home to Deborah soon after their marriage and that Deborah agreed to raise the boy. Deborah not only took care of William, but soon she and Ben had their own child—a boy named Francis.

Tragically, Francis died at the age of four. Vaccinations against smallpox had recently been developed, and Ben had planned to have Francis inoculated as soon as he got over a cold. But before the boy received his shot, he caught the dread disease and died. Many years later Ben wrote that he could still not think of "Franky" without a sigh.

Seven years after Francis's death, Sarah, nicknamed Sally, was born to Deborah and Ben. Though Sally never received from her father as much love

Mrs. Deborah Franklin, engraved by Joseph Andrews. (The Library Company of Philadelphia)

and attention as her half brother William, she was the one who remained the most loyal. Ben's much-adored first son would one day become his enemy, taking up arms against Ben's greatest cause.

Soon after Ben and Deborah were married, they

had opened a store which was then called a stationery shop. The store sold a lot more than stationery supplies, however. It sold books, tea, coffee, cheese, iron stoves, soap, and a variety of other items. The two worked cheerfully together. Deborah called Ben Pappy. She not only raised the children and kept the household in smooth-running order, but she also tended to the stationery store, did the bookkeeping,

Franklin pushing a wheelbarrow full of newspapers through the streets of Philadelphia. (American Philosophical Society)

and folded and stitched pamphlets for Ben's printing business.

Ben was soon the most active printer in the American colonies. When the Pennsylvania Assembly appointed him their official printer, he began printing the colony's paper money, laws, and documents. He also became Public Printer for Delaware, New Jersey, and Maryland. And he helped others establish newspapers in New York, Connecticut, and two islands in the West Indies.

By the time he was thirty, the "poor ignorant boy" whom the governor had tricked had done all right on his own.

Man of the Enlightenment

I was surprised to find myself so much fuller of faults than I had imagined; but I had the satisfaction of seeing them diminish.
—*from* The Autobiography of Benjamin Franklin

During those busy years in Philadelphia, Franklin made a daily schedule for himself. He rose at five in the morning and prayed to "Powerful Goodness"—his name for God. As he planned his day, he always asked, "What good shall I do today?" He then studied and read until eight, when he began work in his printing shop.

After working in his printing and stationery shops until noon, Ben ate lunch and looked at his accounts until two o'clock, at which time he went back to work. At six he had supper. Then he played music and visited with his family and friends until ten. At the end of each evening, he always asked himself, "What good have I done today?"

The supposed site of Franklin's print shop in Philadelphia. (The Library Company of Philadelphia)

Ben's last question of the day was typical of the century in which he lived. Today we call the 1700s the period of the Enlightenment. During the Enlightenment many learned men no longer believed in the absolute power of the church. They believed that God could be found in nature or in man's good sense. For this reason they turned away from organized religions and turned toward the scientific world. These thinkers thought that "real" knowledge about the world was better than superstitious, religious thinking.

Ben Franklin was a shining example of an Enlightenment thinker in many ways. First, he believed in the value of education for ordinary people. He argued in favor of education for women and black people. He was one of the founders of the University of Pennsylvania. Though he'd only had two years of "formal" education himself, he studied and read constantly. He taught himself four foreign languages—Italian, French, Spanish, and Latin. He was the first writer on education to recommend teaching modern languages in school. Always the pragmatist, he also recommended teaching agriculture, science, and athletics.

Ben Franklin also started the first public library in America. He and a group of citizens bought books and opened a lending library in Philadelphia that operated two days a week. Soon other towns began to imitate Franklin's library, until reading became fashionable even among the people who were not well educated.

Men of the Enlightenment were also committed to the idea of working together to improve their communities. Soon after his return from London Franklin formed a club called the Junto. These men were mostly tradesmen, such as silversmiths, printers, shoemakers, and ironmasters. The purpose of the club

The original building of the Library Company, founded by Franklin, in a print by W. Birch done in 1799. (The Library Company of Philadelphia)

was "to do good"—and to make money while they were doing it. The Junto club was able to steer business Franklin's way and also to help him find material for his newspaper. This club gave birth to other American business clubs—such as the Kiwanis, the Lions, and the Rotary clubs of today.

Years later, in 1744, Franklin founded the American Philosophical Society. The learned members of that society corresponded with each other on all

The Philosophical Hall and Independence Hall in Philadelphia. The Philosophical Hall was the home of the American Philosophical Society, which Franklin founded, and was restored to its original design in 1949. (American Philosophical Society)

aspects of nature. They shared new information on farm animals, gardening, trees, medicines, math, chemistry, minerals, maps, and sea charts. Like other men of the Enlightenment, these men were avidly curious about the natural world and wanted to share any information that might help increase man's power over nature.

Many thinkers of the Enlightenment also believed

that people should try to become perfect—not because the church said so—but because it seemed the most *practical* way to be. Ben Franklin was very intent on becoming perfect. He later wrote in his autobiography that he "wished to live without committing any fault at any time." In order to do this he wrote down the thirteen virtues he wished most to have. They were: temperance, silence, order, resolution, frugality, industry, sincerity, justice, moderation, cleanliness, tranquility, chastity, and humility.

One virtue that Ben did not include on his list was patience. Since he wanted to become perfect as quickly as possible, he made a plan to concentrate on one virtue per week. In a special notebook with ivory-colored pages he marked down how well he was doing. All his life he carried the little book with him.

Not only did Ben try to become perfect, but he also spent a great deal of energy trying to teach others how to become perfect. His lessons, however, were not rigid and stern. Rather, they were taught with wonderful humor, in a series of booklets called *Poor Richard's Almanack.*

Almanacs were a favorite form of reading in colonial America. They were small books that forecast the weather and told about the tides and changes of the moon. They also contained calendars, jokes, poems, and odd facts. In 1732 Ben Franklin began

Poor Richard, 1733.

AN

Almanack

For the Year of Chriſt

1 7 3 3,

Being the Firſt after LEAP YEAR:

And makes ſince the Creation	Years
By the Account of the Eaſtern *Greeks*	7241
By the Latin Church, when ☉ ent. ♈	6932
By the Computation of *W.W.*	5742
By the *Roman* Chronology	5682
By the *Jewiſh* Rabbies	5494

Wherein is contained

The Lunations, Eclipſes, Judgment of the Weather, Spring Tides, Planets Motions & mutual Aſpects, Sun and Moon's Riſing and Setting, Length of Days, Time of High Water, Fairs, Courts, and obſervable Days.

Fitted to the Latitude of Forty Degrees, and a Meridian of Five Hours Weſt from *London*, but may without ſenſible Error, ſerve all the adjacent Places, even from *Newfoundland* to *South-Carolina*.

By *RICHARD SAUNDERS*, Philom.

PHILADELPHIA:
Printed and ſold by *B. FRANKLIN*, at the New Printing-Office near the Market.

The Third Impreſſion.

The title page of an early edition of Poor Richard's Almanack. *(The Library Company of Philadelphia)* publishing his own almanac which he called *Poor Richard's Almanack.*

Poor Richard was a gold mine for Ben—after the Bible, it became the most popular reading in the colonies. It came out once a year and was sprinkled with useful information about the weather and stars. The almanac also gave Ben the chance to share his philosophy of self-improvement. He took many of the sayings from ancient writers and rewrote them to make them simple and clear. Today historians believe that the philosophy expressed in *Poor Richard* helped mold the American character, ideas such as:

> God helps those who help themselves.
>
> Early to bed and early to rise
> Makes a man healthy, wealthy, and wise.
>
> When you're good to others, you are best to yourself.
>
> There are no gains without pains.
>
> At the working man's house hunger looks in, but dares not enter.

For the next twenty-five years, as "Poor Richard," Ben Franklin preached his ideals to the American people—the value of hard work, common sense, and self-sufficiency. Today people might think that his methods of trying to solve human problems were a

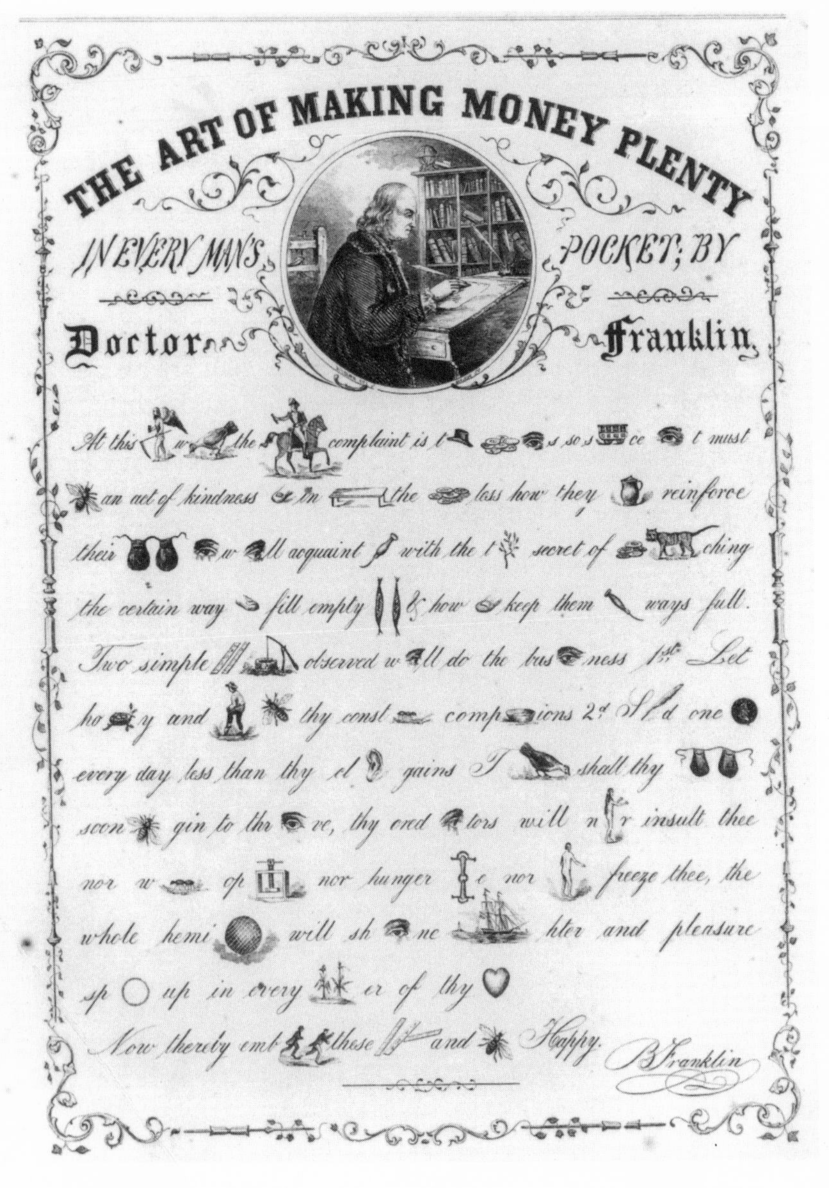

Rebus of the proverbs of Poor Richard, from an almanac published in the 1800s. (The Library Company of Philadelphia)

bit too simple, but Franklin himself seemed to know that. Though he didn't put it on his list, one of his most outstanding virtues was humor. And he seems to be laughing at himself when he writes in *Poor Richard:*

> Who is wise? *He that learns from every one.*
> Who is powerful? *He that governs his passions.*
> Who is rich? *He that is content.*
> Who is that? *Nobody.*

First Citizen of Philadelphia

I began now to turn my thoughts a little to public affairs, beginning, however, with small matters.
—*from* The Autobiography of Benjamin Franklin

WHEN BEN returned to Philadelphia from London in 1726, the city was even larger than New York and Boston. By then Philadelphia was the center of commerce for all the colonies. In spite of its importance, however, it was in great disorder. Community services had not caught up with its rapid growth. The streets were dark and filthy. There were no city policemen, no firemen, no hospitals, no colleges, and no libraries. The city greatly needed organization and planning. And who could be better for that job than Benjamin Franklin?

With the same energy and enthusiasm which he had used to improve himself, Ben set about to improve Philadelphia. He first tackled the problem of fire safety. Since Philadelphians depended upon fireplaces and candles for heat and light, houses frequently caught on fire. Since the houses were close together and often made with wood, the fires spread

Franklin as a fire chief, by C. O. Wright in 1895. (The Historical Society of Philadelphia)

easily, and many buildings burned to the ground. Ben wrote a paper on the city's many fires and read it to his Junto club. The club members responded enthusiastically and helped him form the city's first fire company. The fire company had no fire engine, no sirens, and no hoses. The thirty firemen only had leather water buckets to bring to every fire. But it was a beginning, and soon more fire companies were formed, helping make Philadelphia one of the safest cities in America at that time. Years later Franklin also formed the first fire insurance company in America, and in his old age, he designed a house that was nearly fireproof.

Ben also proposed a plan for cleaning and paving the streets of the city, and for improving its street lamps. He enlisted the help of the Junto to plan a police force, and after he wrote a paper criticizing the local night watchmen for drunkenness and neglect, the town fathers hired men to make up a regular force of watchmen, called the City Watch.

Franklin often showed concern for the disadvantaged. It worried him that a poor widow had to pay as much tax for the City Watch as did a wealthy merchant. So he designed a fair tax system based on a person's income. And years later, when he helped found the first hospital in Pennsylvania "for the Relief of the Sick and Miserable," he proposed that the hospital take care of the poor without charge.

In 1737, Ben was appointed postmaster of Phila-

Franklin helped found the Pennsylvania Hospital in 1751, and this painting was done by John Steeper and Henry Dawkins in 1761. (The Library Company of Philadelphia)

delphia. Soon huge bags of mail were delivered to his shop. The mail not only came from the colonies but from ships that had sailed from Europe and the West Indies. Ben began the service of printing in his newspaper the names of those who had mail waiting at the post office, and after a while, he started a special service in which mail was delivered directly to people's houses. The mailman was called the penny postman because people had to pay a penny for their letters.

In 1753 England appointed Franklin the deputy

postmaster general in North America. At that time the mail service in the colonies was quite poor. Once a week, mailmen picked up the mail from local post offices, such as Ben's printing office. Then they carried the mail on horseback over terrible country roads, heading for the north and south. As deputy postmaster general, Franklin made a three-thousand-mile rugged tour of the postal roads and the ferries that linked the country together. After he studied the problems facing the mail carriers, he was able to increase the frequency of mail service to three deliveries a week. By improving the speed and safety of the mails, he began to draw the colonies together as no one had before.

In 1746 Pennsylvania was the only colony in America that did not have its own volunteer militia. A militia was an army of citizens who were prepared to defend a colony in case of an emergency. The Quakers did not believe in fighting, and since they had a very powerful influence on colony affairs, the citizens of Pennsylvania had never organized their own militia.

But when French and Spanish privateers began attacking settlers along the Delaware River, Franklin felt it was time for action. The city was virtually defenseless against outsiders. So, in a pamphlet called Plain Truth, he argued in favor of a militia. The pamphlet had such a great effect that a meeting was called, and twelve hundred people volunteered to form the guard. It wasn't long before almost ten thousand men had signed up to defend the colony. They were all given arms and assigned to regiments headed by officers; then they met every week to be instructed in military skills. Ben, a leader in the militia, spent a great deal of time acquiring cannons to defend the Delaware River.

The Pennsylvanians soon had other reasons to defend themselves. In 1755 they became involved in a war with the French and Indians. When Pennsylvania had been settled in the late 1600s by the Quakers, William Penn had reported that the Indians were a quiet and peaceful people who hurt no one. Before settlers came from Europe, the Indians had lived in some parts of Pennsylvania for over fifteen thousand years, hunting peacefully and treating the land with great respect. The idea of owning the land puzzled the Indians, for they were accustomed to sharing what they had.

Later, after William Penn's death, his sons in England unjustly claimed the hunting grounds of the Indians. French and English traders also caused terrible drinking problems for the Indians by trading rum and beer for furs with them. Finally, in 1755, after peace had reigned for almost eighty years between the Indians and the English settlers, the Indians felt that they had suffered more injustices than they could bear. The once-friendly tribes joined forces with the French against the English.

The French were angry at the English for their own reasons. At that time the country of France claimed the land of the Ohio Valley. So when an obscure Virginia officer named George Washington brought a message to the French from the governor of Virginia, warning them that the English owned the valley, the French returned the message with insults. Soon afterward fighting broke out. By then the French had convinced the embittered Indians to fight with them. The resulting conflict was called the French and Indian War.

In the face of French and Indian war threats, Franklin wanted all the colonies to unite under an English military governor appointed by King George II. He even conceived the first American political cartoon—a snake cut into sections with the words "Join, or Die" written underneath.

Neither the Pennsylvania colonists nor the English agreed with Ben's proposal. The Pennsylvanians were afraid of being dominated by a royal governor-general, and the English did not want the isolated colonies to be united. King George II preferred to send his own soldiers to fight the French and Indians, for he was afraid that if the colonies were united and strengthened, they might someday try to fight England.

Even though Franklin wanted the colonies to unite, he was not in the least considering a fight with the English. At that time he still thought of England as

The famous political cartoon, first drawn by Franklin, that came to be a symbol of the rebellious colonies. (The Library Company of Philadelphia)

his mother country. After all, his father had come from there, and his ancestors had all been British. So Franklin supported the British soldiers fighting on American soil, and worked hard to raise supplies for them. He bought 259 pack horses and 150 wagons pulled by two horses each. Later he sent rice, raisins, chocolate, coffee, tea, sugar, pepper, biscuits, cheese, hams, butter, rum, and wine to the "redcoats." He was never completely repaid for all the money he spent on supplies.

At one point during the war Franklin was asked to help secure the frontier against horrible Indian attacks. In early December of 1755 Indians had scalped nearly all the settlers in a Moravian village. As Franklin led troops to northeastern Pennsylvania through bitterly cold and rainy weather, he and his son, William, passed through the areas that had been ravaged by the Indians. They saw burned farmhouses and the charred and scalped remains of farmers and their wives and children. Ben and William worked with the local militia to build forts made of wood and earth to help protect the surviving settlers in that region.

Though he had no official military rank and had experienced only fifty days of concentrated military activity, Franklin was called General Franklin by the Moravians. Later, when he returned to the Pennsylvania Assembly, he was officially made a colonel.

No wonder Benjamin Franklin has been called the First Citizen of Philadelphia. He created the first public library, first fire company, first police force, first paved streets, first streetlights, first college, first militia, first foreign-language newspaper, first philosophical society, first hospital, and first fire insurance company. While he did all these things he took care of his growing family and his businesses. He was so successful at his work, that at the age of forty-two, he sold his printing business and dedicated his remaining forty-two years "to doing good."

But soon the First Citizen of Philadelphia would become world-famous—not, however, because he was an outstanding printer, writer, newspaperman, postmaster, politician, or militia colonel. In addition to all of these things, he'd also been inventing, observing, and conducting some of the world's most fantastic scientific experiments.

Scientist and Inventor

As soon as the thunder clouds come over the kite, the pointed wire will draw from them, and the kite with all the twine, will be electrified . . .

—*B. Franklin in* The Pennsylvania Gazette, *Oct. 1752*

IN BEN FRANKLIN'S time the search for new scientific discoveries was like a sport. Because of the Enlightenment, people in the 1700s began to examine their world with less superstition and religious interpretation. One philosopher said it was "as though the very heavens were being opened." At that time little was known about the physical world compared with today. Scientific experiments could be done in one's own home or backyard, rather than in sterile laboratories. Amateurs collected fossils, minerals, insects, and plants. They wrote down what they discovered and compared notes in letters or at club meetings.

Portrait by Chamberlin of Franklin in his study. The bells to his left were fixed so that they would ring when there was lightning in the air. (The Historical Society of Philadelphia)

All his life Ben had been an experimenter and an inventor. He was curious about almost everything in the natural world. The area that excited him the most, however, was the study of electricity. At that time electricity was more of a curiosity than a science.

When showmen traveled through towns, presenting "shocks" to the public, people thought they were seeing magic tricks.

Franklin turned the study of electricity from a parlor game into a science. He started his first electrical experiments in 1743, working at home with a special jar called a Leyden jar. Coated with metal foil, the Leyden jar was a primitive condenser that provided a way to "store" an electrical charge.

After Ben acquired Leyden jars, his house filled with friends who'd come to see his experiments. As usual he had a sense of humor about what he was doing. He once wrote to a friend about an "electrical party" he was planning. He said that the turkey would be killed by electrical shock, then roasted by a fire kindled by electricity. Then the healths of all the famous electricians in Europe were to be drunk to under the firing of guns from an electrical battery.

Franklin wrote about his many experiments in a booklet called *Experiments and Observations on Electricity, Made at Philadelphia in America.* This booklet excited scientists all over Europe. Many set about trying to prove or disprove his findings.

Gradually Ben began to believe that electricity was a force that pervaded the universe. He wondered if lightning might not be part of that same force. Up until that time, lightning had been the terror of the ages. It was a mysterious and awesome force that most people believed was a punishment from God.

But Franklin wanted to prove that lightning and electricity were manifestations of the same force.

Finally he came up with a way to test his theory. One stormy day in 1752, he and his twenty-one-year-old son, William, took a Leyden jar and a silk kite from Ben's laboratory. They crept into a barn

Franklin and his son William making the great kite experiment are shown in a bronze bas-relief on the base of Greenough's statue of Franklin in front of City Hall in Boston. Photographed by Baldwin Coolidge. (American Philosophical Society)

in a secluded field where no one could see them, for Ben was afraid he would be mocked if his experiment failed. People might say, "Oh yes, crazy Franklin is now flying a child's kite in a storm—"

But Ben's kite was no ordinary child's kite. His kite had a silk ribbon attached to the end of its string. Since silk did not conduct electricity, Franklin thought the ribbon would protect him from getting electrocuted—at least he hoped it would. He wasn't sure, for no one knew all the mysterious things that could happen when one played with electricity. Franklin had been knocked unconscious twice during other experiments.

Another unusual feature of Franklin's kite was a small metal key attached to the kite string. This is where Ben hoped to see the electricity spark. As the storm raged about them Franklin kept touching the key to see if it gave him a small shock. But nothing happened—the key remained cold.

Ben and William were close to giving up when suddenly the threads of the kite string stood on end. Ben touched the key, and he felt the familiar jolt of electricity! He quickly picked up his Leyden jar and touched its wire to the key. The electricity then poured down the wet string to the key and into the Leyden jar. Ben Franklin had proved his theory—lightning and electricity were one and the same!

Franklin next set about to make practical use of his discovery. In colonial America, buildings were always in danger of being struck by lightning and burning to the ground. Perhaps now that he had proved that electricity and lightning were parts of the same force, lightning could be brought under control so that it would no longer destroy houses and barns. Wouldn't a tall iron rod serve the same purpose as his kite string? If the rod was attached to the side of a house, then when the lightning struck, the electricity in the lightning would pass through the metal down into the ground—just as it had passed down the kite string into the Leyden jar. Then nothing would catch on fire.

Ben shared his new theories in the next *Poor Richard's Almanack*, and soon houses and barns all over Pennsylvania became protected by lightning rods. By drawing the lightning down into the earth, the rods saved thousands of buildings from fire and destruction.

It may seem odd to us today, but many people in Franklin's time feared that it might be wrong to stop houses from being hit by lightning. Although interest in scientific discoveries was very great, so little of the cause of things was known that people still worried about interfering with God's plans. They wondered if lightning rods would make God angry. Even Franklin's own Junto club debated the question: "May we place rods on our houses to guard them from lightning without being guilty of presumption?"

Ben Franklin's reputation as a great scientist spread quickly. The popular view was that he was more than a scientist—he was also a wizard and a holy man. He soon became known far and wide as the man who snatched lightning down from the sky.

Sometimes Franklin enjoyed his reputation for being a wizard. Once, on a walk, he fooled a group of friends by telling them he could calm the waters as Christ had. He then raised his cane over a rippling pond and waved it in the air as if making magic letters. Suddenly—miraculously—the pond became glassy and still. The crowd was stunned.

Ben later confessed the water had become calm for a scientific reason and not a religious one. Once when he'd crossed the ocean, he'd noticed that an oil lantern swinging out from the ship had caused an area of water to become still. The lamp's oil must have a calming effect on water he thought. So, in order to fool his friends, he had filled his hollow bamboo cane with oil. Then when he waved the cane over the pond, about a teaspoonful dripped out, producing instant calm over a space of several yards.

Benjamin Franklin was always observing the world with intense curiosity and careful attention. On his first trip across the Atlantic he kept a journal, recording information about dolphins, tiny seaweed crabs, storms, ocean temperatures, and eclipses of the moon. He later studied the behavior of ants and pigeons. And on a sunny day he laid different col-

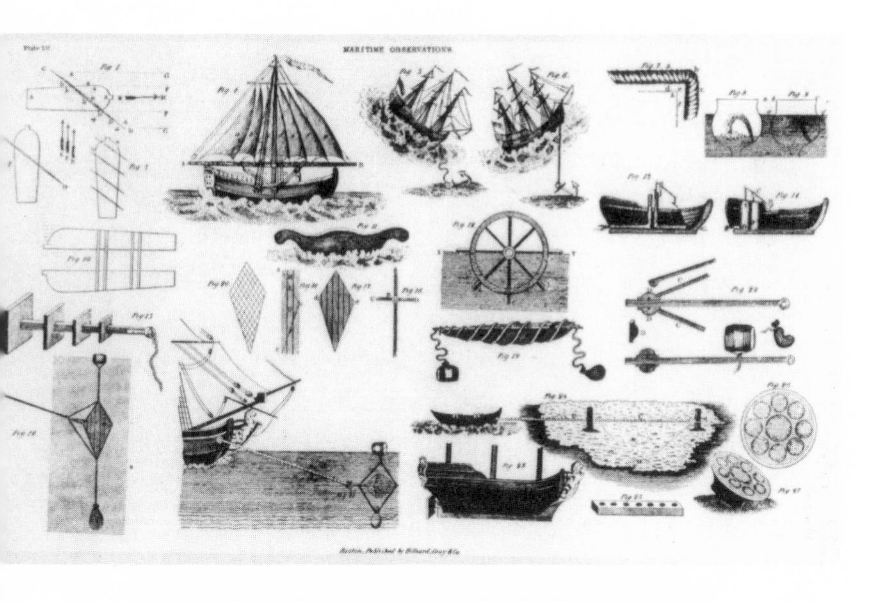

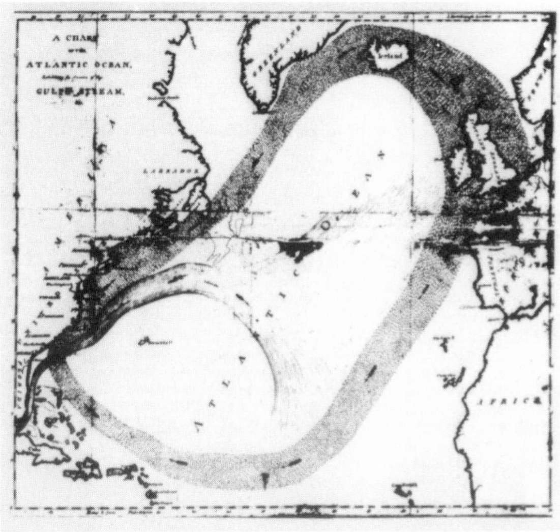

Top: *Maritime observations, including Franklin's sketches for designs of ships and anchors.* Bottom: *Franklin's map of the Gulf Stream. (American Philosophical Society)*

ored cloths upon the snow to demonstrate the different effects of heat on light and dark surfaces. He explained waterspouts at sea, eclipses of the sun, and the origins of northeastern storms. He wrote an important essay on population. He promoted the first American expedition to explore the Arctic, and he studied ancient mastodon tusks and teeth.

Franklin also realized that the nation's resources were not going to last forever. He advised that they should be carefully managed for the sake of future generations.

Along with doing experiments and making discoveries, Franklin invented bifocals, a glass armonica, and a new kind of ship's anchor. He devised a mechanical arm for removing books from high shelves. He made a candle from whale oil that made a clear white light and lasted much longer than tallow candles. He invented an armchair that could be transformed into library steps. He once put together a pulley system to lock and unlock his bedroom door from his bed. And Ben's bathroom probably had the first flush toilet in America.

Perhaps one of his most famous inventions was his wood stove. Not only did the stove have an open place for the firebox so that people could enjoy the sight of the fire, but it sent heat into the room instead of allowing it to escape up the chimney. Since the Franklin stove, as it was called, doubled

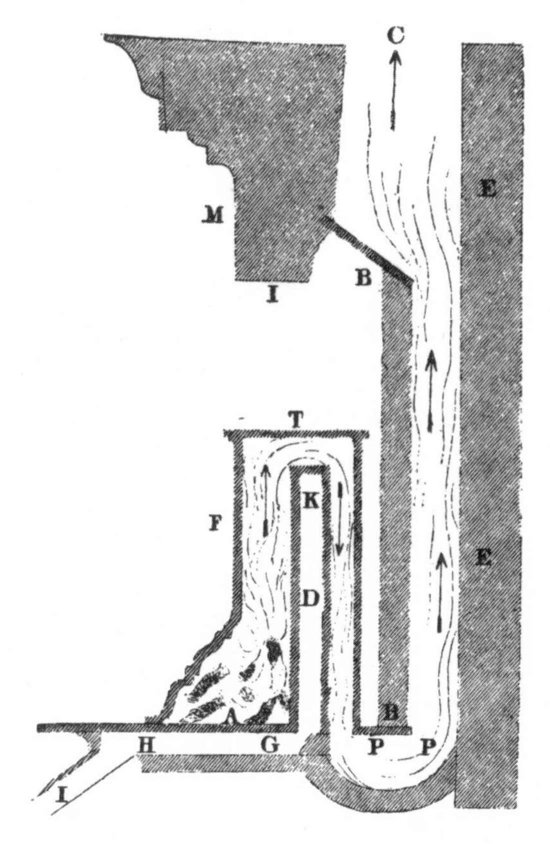

The Franklin stove. (American Philosophical Society)

the amount of heat given off by any other stove, it used a lot less fuel.

For his scientific work Ben Franklin won recognition from learned people all over the world. In 1753 London's Royal Society, the elite of England's scientific organizations, unanimously elected him a member and awarded him the Copley medal, its

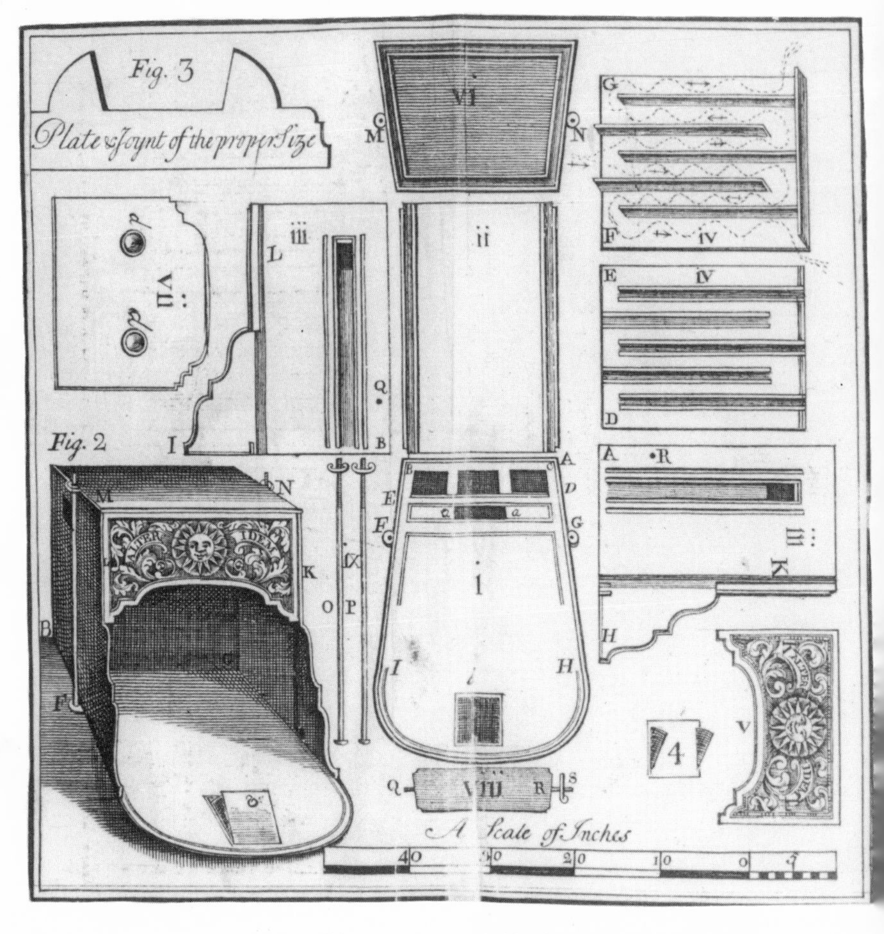

An engraving of Franklin's stove, probably by James Turner, after Lewis Evans. (The Library Company of Philadelphia)

highest award. The Royal Academy of Sciences in Paris and the Royal Society of Sciences in Hanover, Germany, both elected him as a member. He was honored by the Academies of Arts and Sciences in Orleans and Lyons, France, and was elected a fellow

The library chair invented by Franklin with the steps hidden in the seat that can be pulled out and used to reach tall shelves. (American Philosophical Society)

of the American Academy of Arts and Sciences and a member of the Academy of Science, Letters, and Arts of Padua, Italy. In a short period of time, Ben Franklin became the best-known American in Europe.

Though he received many honors for his work, Franklin chose not to make money from any of his inventions. He could have made a fortune on the lightning rod and the Franklin stove alone. Other men later patented his ideas and did make fortunes. But Ben chose to give his inventions to the world freely, as a way of thanking other inventors. In a

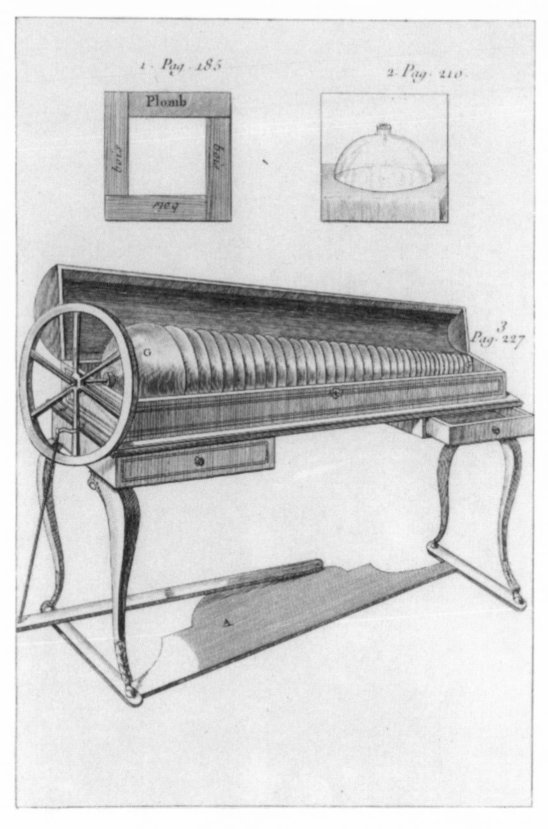

The armonica, a musical instrument invented by Franklin, inspired by the glass harmonica. The player pumps the foot pedal, which turns the glasses, and places wet fingers on the spinning glass to produce a tone, just like rubbing a wet finger on a drinking glass.
(The Houghton Library, Harvard University)

letter to his mother he said that when he died, he'd rather it be said, "He lived usefully," than, "He died rich."

Franklin even speculated at one time on how to raise the dead. In a letter to a friend he told of seeing drowned flies revived by exposure to the sun. He wondered if persons could ever be revived in the same way. He wished that he himself could be brought back someday from the dead, for he had a strong "desire to see and observe the state of America a hundred years hence."

Agent to England

Our Assembly talk of sending me to England speedily. Then look out sharp, and if a fat old fellow should come to your Printing House and request a little Smouting (part-time work) depend on it, 'tis your affectionate friend and humble servant.
—B. Franklin, in a letter to an English friend

WILLIAM PENN, the gentle Quaker leader, had thought of Pennsylvania as a "holy experiment," or as a haven for persecuted men. But after Penn died, his sons, Thomas and Richard, who lived mainly in England, became the proprietors of Pennsylvania, and they saw the faraway land only as a source of income. The independent-minded colony grew angry with the Penns' control over them, and in 1757, they sent their colonial agent, Ben Franklin, to England to settle various disputes with the Penns.

When he set sail in the spring of 1757, little did Franklin realize he would be spending fifteen of the

A portrait of Franklin in his fifties, from a painting by Benjamin Wilson done in 1759. (The Library Company of Philadelphia)

next seventeen years of his life in England. Traveling with him was twenty-six-year-old William Franklin. Ben and William were more like brothers than father and son. They had captured lightning together. They'd ridden side by side as soldiers in the French and Indian War. Now William would serve as his father's secretary during Ben's mission as agent for Pennsylvania.

Deborah Franklin didn't go on the journey, and neither did their daughter Sally. Deborah was terrified of sea voyages, for in those days trips across the ocean took many weeks and were often dangerous. On this particular voyage Ben's ship was nearly wrecked against some rocks in the middle of the night.

When the light from a lighthouse warned the ship's captain and saved everyone, the always-practical Franklin decided he must encourage the building of more lighthouses in America.

When they arrived in London, Ben and William rented rooms from a warm, spunky widow named Mrs. Stevenson. She kindly nursed Ben when he was deliriously ill for eight weeks with fever and terrible head pain. Thereafter she became a lifelong friend. Ben also lavished much attention and affection on his landlady's daughter, Polly Stevenson. Since his own daughter, Sally, was far away, Polly became a substitute daughter for him. The two remained very good friends for over thirty years, until Polly stood by his bedside as he lay dying.

In the Stevenson house Ben set up electrical apparatus in one of his rooms, and people flocked from everywhere to see his experiments. He played the harp and violin on musical evenings with his friends. He swam in the Thames River and took his daily "air baths." He firmly believed that fresh air kept away illness. Every morning—even in winter—he opened all the windows in his room and sat nude for an hour or so.

Meanwhile Ben and Deborah wrote many letters back and forth across the Atlantic. He often addressed her as "My dear child . . ." And he pleaded with her to join him in London. But Deborah's fear of sea travel kept her at home.

While Deborah wrote letters full of advice on how Ben should take better care of himself, he sent many things back to her from England. It was as if he were trying to share the elegance of English life with his family. He sent fine crystal, silverware, silk blankets, silver cups, and satin cloaks. To most Americans at that time Benjamin Franklin's name meant simplicity and thriftiness. But he was more complicated than that, for he enjoyed the finer things in life too.

In spite of Ben's disputes with the Penns, he and William had a wonderful time abroad. Not only did they enjoy the rich cultural life of London, but they also traveled to the village of Ecton where for two centuries or more the Franklin family had lived on a thirty-acre farm. Ben and William must have been very moved when they visited the decayed old stone building known as the "Franklin House," and when they stepped into the old forge near the house where many generations of their forefathers had worked as blacksmiths. As father and son wandered through England they had no idea of the terrible conflict that would divide the two of them forever. Neither did they know that William's ever-growing love for England would be the source of that conflict.

But for now, Ben and William happily frequented taverns and coffee shops together. They dined with politicians, and Ben exchanged letters with scientists and thinkers. He wrote numerous newspaper articles and letters under pen names, such as "A Briton," "A New Englandman," "A Spectator," and "A Traveller." When an Englishman wrote an article that criticized the colonists for their dress, language, and fighting abilities, Ben answered humorously, pointing out that all these things had come to America from England.

These years were also rich in honors for Franklin. In 1759 he and William journeyed to Scotland where he was awarded the title of doctor by the University of St. Andrews. It was an honor he was especially pleased with, since he had not had more than two years of formal schooling in his life. Thereafter he always liked to be called Doctor Franklin.

In 1762, after being away for five years, Ben finally settled matters with the Penns and returned to America. Deborah, overjoyed to be with him again, was soon busy helping him plan a new house for their family.

But their building plans were soon brought to a halt by political problems in the Pennsylvania government. Ben was very upset when a peaceful group of Indians was slaughtered by a gang of farmers called the Paxton Boys. The gang had killed the Indians in order to revenge settlers who'd been attacked by other Indians. Ben wrote the most moving pamphlet of his life, defending the slain Indians:

What had little boys and girls done; what could children of a year old, babes at the breast, what could they do, that they too must be shot and hatcheted? . . . and in their parents' arms! This is done by no civilized nation in Europe. Do we come to America to learn and practice the manners of barbarians?

A political cartoon at the time of the Paxton Boys rebellion, showing Franklin on the right, wearing glasses, being whispered to by the devil. (The Library Company of Philadelphia)

When the Paxton Boys, now a crowd of three hundred, marched on Philadelphia to attack more Indians, the Governor ran to Franklin's house at midnight for advice. Franklin advised the city to confront the Paxtons. And the next day, he and others met with them and reached an agreement. Of this episode Franklin later wrote to a friend: "Within four and twenty hours, your old friend was a common soldier, a counsellor, a kind of dictator, an ambassador to the country mob, and on their returning home, nobody, again."

The pamphlet Ben wrote defending the Indians won him more enemies than friends, and was partly responsible for his losing his seat in the Pennsylvania Assembly. The slaughter of the innocent Indians caused further problems between the Penns in England and the Pennsylvania colonists. So, in the fall of 1764, although Franklin was not an elected member of the Assembly, he was asked to return to England and present a petition to the king, requesting this time a complete end to the Penns' power in the colony.

But not long after Ben arrived in England, *all* the colonies began having trouble with England's control over them. As Sally Franklin wrote to her father from America: "The subject now is the Stamp Act and nothing else is talked of. . . ."

The Stamp Act was a special tax that England wanted to place on the colonies, for King George III wanted the colonists to help pay for the French and Indian War. For the first time the colonists would have to pay taxes directly to England on newspa-

King George III of England. (Historical Society of Philadelphia)

pers, legal documents, and many other items. In the past, they'd always voted on their own taxes.

The colonists were furious. "Taxation without representation is tyranny!" they cried. They should not have to pay the Stamp Tax, they thought, for they were not even represented in the English Parliament. In Boston mobs took to the streets and smashed the houses of the stamp officer and the lieutenant governor.

In Philadelphia Franklin's enemies pointed the finger at Ben across the ocean and accused him of taking part in creating the Stamp Act. When angry rioters threatened to attack the Franklin home, Deborah behaved fearlessly. With the help of her cousin and brother, she gathered several guns and turned the house into a fortress. When asked to move out, she staunchly declared that Ben had not done anything to hurt anyone, nor had she. The rioters finally backed down, and the night ended peacefully.

Not only did Franklin not help create the Stamp Act—but in London he fought night and day against it. He printed a political cartoon making fun of it, and he bombarded London newspapers with sarcastic letters. In February, 1766, he spoke before the British House of Commons. After he identified himself as "Franklin of Philadelphia," he answered 174 questions about the Stamp Act and the colonies. He spoke with such reason, clarity, and dignity that a week later the hated tax was repealed.

When the news reached Philadelphia, there was wild rejoicing. Sally wrote to Ben that people rang bells and made bonfires. Up and down the east coast, in taverns and coffeehouses, Ben Franklin was hailed a hero. Three hundred men in the Pennsylvania State House toasted him as well.

After the repeal of the Stamp Act, the Pennsylvania Assembly reappointed Franklin as their agent. Within a few years, he was asked to be agent for Georgia, New Jersey, and Massachusetts. For nine years he was the voice of the American colonies in England. He worked tirelessly, writing articles and pamphlets and organizing meetings and petitions—until the British government, enraged by the Boston Tea Party, decided to thoroughly disgrace him.

EXPLANATION

The above Prophetical Emblem, of what would be the Miserable State of Great Britain and her Colonies, Should She persist in restraining their Trade, destroying their Currency, and Taxing their People by Laws made by a Legislature, where they are not Represented.

The Author, with a Sagacity and Invention natural to himself, has comprized in one View, under the Character of Belisarius, the late Flourishing State of Great Britain, in the Zenith of Glory and Honour, with her Fall into the most Abject State of Disgrace Misery and Ruin. Belisarius was one of the Greatest Heroes of the Antients. He lived under Justinian the Emperor; He Gain'd a Victory over and concluded an Honourable Peace with Cabades King of Persia, Took Carthage and Subdued Gilimer the Usurper of the Crown of the Vandals, Overthrew Vitigas and refused the Throne of the Goths when offer'd to him; Rebuilt the Walls of Rome after they were destroy'd by Totila, and performed many other Military Atchievments too tedious to enumerate. In this Part of his Character is represented the late Successful and Flourishing State of Great Britain, which Aided the King of Prussia against the Powerful Armies of Hungary and Russia; Supported Portugal against the Spaniards, and reduc'd France and Spain to the most Advantageous Terms of Accommodation.

By the latter Part of Belisarius's Life is represented the Unhappy and Miserable State of Great Britain, should the late Measures against America take Place. This General at length being Accused of a Conspiracy against Justinian, That Emperor barbarously Ordered his Eyes to be pulled out, which reduced him to the Greatest Poverty, and Obliged him to Subsist on the Alms of others. The Motto is also Striking, and elegantly Expressive of this Truth Date Obolum Belisario Give Poor Belisarius a Penny.

View the Countenance of Great Britain under this Character, and you Perceive nothing but Abject Despondency: Her Eyes, and the Stumps of her mangled Arms raised towards Heaven in Vain. Behold her Colonies, the Source of Her Commerce, Wealth and Glory, Separated from her Body, and no longer Useful to her. The Famous English Oak Deprived of its Wide Extended Top and late flourishing Branches, save a few, and those with its Body withered and Decay'd. The Ground beneath it producing nothing but Bryars and Thorns. The British Ships, the Instruments of her Trade, with Brooms on their Topmasts, denoting that they are Advertized for Sale, being no longer either necessary or Useful to her People. Her Shield which she is incapable of Wielding, laying useless by her. The Laurel Branch dropping from the hand of Pennsylvania, which She is rendered unable to retain. And in Fine, Britania herself Sliding off the World, no longer Courted by the Powers of Europe; No longer Able to Sustain its Ballance; No longer respected or Known among Nations.

Moral.

The Political Moral of this Picture is Now easily discovered. History affords us many Instances, of the Ruin of States, by the Prosecution of Measures, ill Suited to the Temper and Genius of its People. The Ordaining of Laws in favour of one Part of the Nation, to the Prejudice and Oppression of Another, is certainly the most erroneous & Mistaken Policy. An Equal Dispensation of Protection Rights Priviledges and Advantages, is what any Part is entitled to, and ought to enjoy: It being a Matter of no Moment to the State whether a Subject grows Rich and flourishing on the Thames or the Ohio, in Edinburgh or Dublin. These Measures Never fail to Create great and Violent Jealousies and Animosities between the People favoured and the People Oppressed. From whence a total Separation of Affections, Interests, Political Obligations and all manner of Connections necessarily Ensue, by which the whole State is Weakened and perhaps ruined forever. ———

Engraved in Philadelphia

A political cartoon drawn by Franklin in 1766, of a maimed England with her colonies cut off because of the Stamp Act. He had this cartoon printed and handed to the members of Parliament during the debates about the repeal of the Stamp Act. (The Library Company of Philadelphia)

In December of 1773, a group of Bostonians, dressed up as Indians, stormed aboard three British ships in the Boston harbor and dumped three hundred chests of tea into the sea to protest the new tax on tea. The English government decided to take out their revenge in part on Ben Franklin. He'd recently been charged with another matter—of giving controversial letters to the Massachusetts government. But after the Boston Tea Party, King George III and his Privy Council wanted blood. So Ben was called before the council to be reprimanded.

Wearing a velvet coat and a long, old-fashioned wig, he stood as still as a rock for an hour as the British lawyer sneeringly attacked him, calling him a common thief and a man without honor. As the lawyer raged against him, Franklin kept a tranquil expression on his face. His self-control must have been one of the greatest achievements of his life, for, as he listened, he saw the end of nine years of his work.

The next day Franklin was stripped of his royal post as deputy postmaster general of North America. It was a bitter and humiliating loss. Not only did he lose a major source of income, but he also lost all chance to help America in England. As he watched Britain close the port of Boston to punish Americans for the Boston Tea Party, his contempt for the British government deepened.

To make matters worse, within the year Franklin

A European engraving of the Boston Tea Party by Daniel-Nicholas Chodowiecki in 1784. (The Library Company of Philadelphia)

Franklin in the Cockpit, a chamber of Parliament in London, being questioned and mocked about the Boston Tea Party. (American Philosophical Society)

lost his most loyal friend—his wife, Deborah. She died of a stroke in December, 1774, without having seen her husband for the last ten years.

It was time to go home.

The Oldest Revolutionary

Figure to yourself an old man, with grey hair appearing under a Martin fur cap, among the powder'd heads of Paris.

—B. Franklin in a letter to a friend, 1777

WHILE BEN FRANKLIN was sailing home from England, British redcoats and American colonists began killing each other. The British soldiers, who had been sent to America to keep order, fought the patriots in the villages of Lexington and Concord, Massachusetts, on April 19, 1775. More colonists then joined to form an army, as farmers and merchants alike picked up their muskets and headed for battle. By the time Franklin reached Philadelphia in May, 1775, the Revolutionary War had truly begun.

Franklin immediately began to help organize the revolution. Within a day he was elected as a delegate to the second Continental Congress. When he had been in England, the first Continental Congress had met, at which time the delegates had agreed to stop importing British goods. The meeting this time, however, was about going to war, and General George Washington was elected the "Commander in Chief of the entire army of the United Colonies."

An ornamental detail from a map from the early 1800s, showing Franklin and Washington. (The Library Company of Philadelphia)

The next year and a half were the busiest of Franklin's life. Though at sixty-nine he was the Congress's oldest member, he had the revolutionary fire of a young man. He served on no fewer than ten committees and was known as a wise man who did not waste words. Thomas Jefferson, the young Virginia delegate, later wrote of Franklin and Washington: "I never heard either of them speak ten minutes at a time, nor to any but the main point which was to decide the question. They laid their shoulders to the great points, knowing the little ones would follow of themselves."

During that time Franklin gathered lead and gunpowder for the American army. When he was appointed America's first postmaster general, he donated his salary to wounded soldiers. As postmaster general, he drew up plans for a new postal service, which helped the war news travel more quickly.

In the fall of 1775 Ben and two other committee members met with General Washington at his camp outside Boston. The three men helped the commander in chief plan a better army. They devised ways to gather more supplies and maintain better discipline.

The following spring Ben went to Canada to try to win support for the colonists there. He and others took a grueling journey that lasted nearly a month. Though seventy years old, Ben traveled in an open flatboat through ice and snow. On land again, he traveled over bad roads and slept in the woods, hungry and cold. His legs swollen, his skin covered with boils, he nearly collapsed with exhaustion. When only a handful of Canadians could be won over to the American cause, he returned home in despair. "The army must starve, plunder, or surrender," he wrote.

Ben must have also been grieving for his son William. For, despite all his efforts, William Franklin sided with the British against the American colonists. In June of 1776, William, then the governor of New Jersey, was arrested for being an "enemy of

Franklin's son William as Governor of New Jersey. (The Historical Society of Philadelphia)

this country." William was put in jail in Connecticut. After his arrest, he and Ben never saw each other again, except for one time after the war. The great wound between them was never healed, as evidenced in a passage Ben wrote to William years later:

> *. . . indeed nothing has ever hurt me so much and affected me with such keen sensations, as to find myself deserted in my old age by my only son; and not only deserted, but to find him taking up arms against me, in a cause wherein my good fame, my fortune, and life were all at stake.*

The American colonists continued to fight, in spite of the odds against them. In June, 1776, a committee was set up to draft the Declaration of Independence—the document that would claim America to be a completely separate nation from England.

The declaration was primarily the work of Thomas Jefferson. But in several places Franklin made the writing simpler and more precise. When it was first read in Philadelphia on July 8, 1776, the Liberty Bell clanged. Then the British royal coat of arms was torn from the statehouse wall and burned. When the declaration was signed in August, Franklin reportedly said, "Gentlemen, we must now all hang together, or most assuredly we shall hang separately."

In the fall of 1776, as the British occupied New York with a well-equipped army, they outnumbered the ragged little army of General Washington two to one. The American colonies had little money, no weapons manufacturer, no navy, and very few trained soldiers. They desperately needed help from abroad. And the country most likely to help them was France.

A Declaration by the Representatives of the UNITED STATES OF AMERICA, in General Congress assembled.

When in the course of human events it becomes necessary for one people to dissolve the political bands which have connected them with another, and to assume among the powers of the earth the separate and equal station to which the laws of nature & of nature's god entitle them, a decent respect to the opinions of mankind requires that they should declare the causes which impel them to the separation.

We hold these truths to be self-evident; that all men are created equal; that they are endowed by their creator with [inherent &] inalienable rights; that among these are life, liberty, & the pursuit of happiness; that to secure these rights, governments are instituted among men, deriving their just powers from the consent of the governed; that whenever any form of government becomes destructive of these ends, it is the right of the people to alter or to abolish it, & to institute new government, laying it's foundation on such principles & organising it's powers in such form, as to them shall seem most likely to effect their safety & happiness. prudence indeed will dictate that governments long established should not be changed for light & transient causes: and accordingly all experience hath shewn that mankind are more disposed to suffer while evils are sufferable, than to right themselves by abolishing the forms to which they are accustomed. but when a long train of abuses & usurpations [begun at a distinguished period &] pursuing invariably the same object, evinces a design to reduce them under absolute Despotism, it is their right, it is their duty, to throw off such government & to provide new guards for their future security. such has been the patient sufferance of these colonies; & such is now the necessity which constrains them to [expunge] alter their former systems of government. the history of the present king of Great Britain is a history of [unremitting] repeated injuries and usurpations, [among which, appears no solitary fact to contradict the uniform tenor of the rest, but all have] in direct object the establishment of an absolute tyranny over these states. to prove this, let facts be submitted to a candid world, [for the truth of which we pledge a faith yet unsullied by falsehood.]

A draft of the Declaration of Independence, with editing by Franklin. (Library of Congress)

The French monarchy was still angry at the English for defeating them in the French and Indian war. French citizens were in favor of the American cause because it impressed them to see such a small and ill-equipped country defy a powerful king. They themselves had long been oppressed by an unfair monarchy where the entire tax burden fell on the poor. But at the beginning of the American Revolution, the French were afraid to come out in the open and help the American cause, for this would mean that they were declaring war against England.

Congress asked Ben Franklin and two others to travel to France and try to win aid for their cause. Ben invited his two grandsons, sixteen-year-old Temple and seven-year-old Benny, to go with him. Then he lent the Congress some of his own money, left his papers in safekeeping, and he and the boys took off for France on a three-masted sailing ship.

It was a long and unpleasant sea journey. Franklin's boils broke out again. The waves were rough, and he was confined most of the day to his cramped cabin with only salt beef and biscuits to eat. In spite of his discomfort, he braved the wet, windy cold to go outside and take daily temperature readings of the Gulf Stream.

When Ben Franklin, the best-known American in Europe, arrived in France, he was treated with great adulation. Wearing spectacles, a coonskin hat, a plain brown suit, and carrying a crab-apple–tree walking stick, Dr. Franklin looked like a backwoods hero. To the French in their powdered wigs and silk coats, he seemed brilliant, simple, and free. One Frenchman wrote: "Such a person was made to excite the curiosity of Paris. The people clustered around as he passed and asked, 'Who is this old peasant who has such a noble air?' "

Franklin in Paris at the age of 71, in his famous fur cap. (The Library Company of Philadelphia)

Famous French scientists and writers wined and dined him. Sculptors modeled busts of him in marble and bronze. Painters painted portraits of him, and other artists made prints and statuettes of his likeness. His face was on watches, vases, handkerchiefs, dishes, and even pocketknives. "Over here my face has become as common as that of the moon . . ." he wrote.

A French engraving from 1780 showing Diogenes with his lamp, who at last has found his honest man, Benjamin Franklin. (The Library Company of Philadelphia)

A master diplomat, Franklin used his great popularity in France to win friends for America. He recruited help for Washington's army by sending over two of the most valuable officers in the revolution. They were the Marquis de Lafayette and General Baron von Steuben. Lafayette, serving without pay, helped raise supplies for the American army. And Baron von Steuben did a magnificent job training Washington's troops at Valley Forge.

Ever cheerful and witty, Franklin kept bad war news from the French. He wanted them to believe America had a good chance of winning the conflict. For the French would not declare war on England until it was proven to them that the Americans could win.

The victory that Franklin was waiting for came in October, 1777, when the patriots won the Battle of Saratoga, in which nearly five thousand redcoats were taken prisoner by the Americans. That victory was the turning point of the Revolutionary War, for on February 6th, 1778, Franklin and King Louis XVI signed the Treaty of Alliance. Later, Spain and Holland also declared war on England.

After a hard winter at Valley Forge, Washington's army greeted the news of the Treaty of Alliance with great joy and celebration. The news temporarily lifted their spirits and encouraged them to continue the fight.

Shortly after the signing of the treaty, Franklin

and other delegates were formally received by the king at his palace. This was the final stamp of approval from the French. When Franklin arrived at the French court, he shocked everyone as he stepped from his coach. Fashion at Louis XVI's court was strictly regulated. A man had to wear formal attire, including a wig and a sword. When Franklin stepped into the courtyard, he wore only his plain brown suit and his spectacles. His hair hung loosely above his shoulders, and he carried a simple white hat under his arm. The crowd gasped with fright and admiration. They thought the American was being too daring for his own good. The king's chamberlain even hesitated before letting him into the king's presence.

But King Louis XVI did not seem to mind the way Franklin was dressed. As soon as he saw the diplomat dressed in simple Quaker garb, he greeted him with warmth, then assured him he would support the American cause. It is reported that he said, "Firmly assure Congress of my friendship. I hope this will be for the good of the two nations."

Perhaps the king would not have been so enthusiastic if he could have seen into his own future, for thirteen years later, encouraged by the American example, the French people overturned the dictatorship of King Louis XVI during the French Revolution, and both the king and his wife were guillotined.

After the treaty was signed, Franklin concentrated

Franklin being presented to the French king, Louis XVI, engraved by Daniel-Nicholas Chodowiecki in 1784. (The Library Company of Philadelphia)

on helping the American navy. He arranged to refit damaged American ships, and he sent over French ships to threaten the British supply lines. When Franklin helped secure a ship for the brilliant young American naval officer, John Paul Jones, in gratitude, Jones named the ship *Bon Homme Richard*—after Franklin's Poor Richard.

Franklin also worked very hard to obtain loans from the French for Washington's desperate army. Since

Franklin surrounded by the ladies of the French court, from an engraving by W. O. Gellar, after the painting by Baron Jolly. (American Philosophical Society)

the United States at that time was nothing more than an unorganized group of different colonies, it did not have a real government. People did not even pay taxes or use the same currency. So Franklin continually had to beg France for more money to help the patriots fight the war.

France gave huge sums of money to the Americans, and also sent over large shipments of war supplies, food, and clothing. It was many months, however, before these supplies reached General Washington's army, for they not only had to be slipped past the British naval blockade, but they had to be transported over terrible roads as well.

Even though the Treaty of Alliance had been signed, for the next three years the embattled Americans suffered hardship after hardship. About one fifth of the army was barefoot, and many men only wore rags. In 1781 over a thousand soldiers mutinied, demanding that they at least be paid for their service.

Finally, however, in the summer of 1781 an army of soldiers arrived from France to help the patriots. At that time the British were in the south, taking possession of the countryside and working their way north. General Washington and his army marched with an army of French troops to Yorktown, Virginia, and there, in September, a force of 8,000 Americans and 7,800 French attacked and captured the fortress of the British commander, General Charles Cornwallis.

Finally, on October 17, 1781, the English were forced to wave a white flag. Two days later they formally surrendered, passing between rows of American and French troops. The French wore their impeccable white uniforms as they stood beside the ragged but proud American soldiers.

After General Cornwallis surrendered at Yorktown, Ben Franklin was appointed to the American Peace Commission. He and others began negotiating with England, until finally, in 1783, a treaty of peace was signed. England now fully agreed to recognize America's independence.

After the treaty of peace was signed, Ben stayed in Paris and negotiated commercial treaties with Sweden and Prussia. Then he finally wrote to Congress, asking that he be allowed to return home. He said he wished "for the little time I have left to be my own master."

Congress agreed to bring Franklin home and appointed Thomas Jefferson, the young Virginian who had written the Declaration of Independence, to replace him in Paris. Jefferson stated that he was only Franklin's successor—for no one, he said, could replace Benjamin Franklin.

After a week of farewell ceremonies, in the late summer of 1785, Ben set sail for home. It was his eighth trip across the Atlantic. Even though he was seventy-nine years old, he was more curious than ever about the world. On the way home he again took notes on the ocean's currents, and on the colors of seaweed. He wrote about fire, lightning, icebergs, Eskimo kayaks, Indian canoes, sailors' diets, lifeboats, shipwrecks, the evils of slavery, and he wrote a lengthy paper called "On the Causes and Cure of Smoky Chimneys."

Ben Franklin's arrival back in Philadelphia is best described by his own journal entry, dated September 14, 1785:

> . . . *we landed at Market Street wharf, where we were received by a crowd of people with huzzas, and accompanied with acclamations quite to my door. Found my family well. God be praised and thanked for all His mercies!*

Founding Father

Let us sit till the Evening of Life is spent; the last hours were always the most joyous. When we can stay no longer 'tis time enough then to bid each other good night, separate, and go quietly to bed.

—B. Franklin in a letter to a friend

BEN FRANKLIN was seventy-nine years old when he returned to Pennsylvania. Upon his arrival, bells rang, and a week of ceremonies welcomed him home. Though he was a citizen of the world now, he still considered Philadelphia his lifelong neighborhood. "The affectionate welcome I met with from my fellow citizens was far beyond my expectation," he wrote. The Pennsylvanian Assembly soon chose him to be President (or governor) of the Commonwealth of Pennsylvania, and he served in this office for three consecutive terms.

Upon his return, Ben moved in with his daughter

A portrait of Franklin from 1787. (The Library Company of Philadelphia)

Sally and her husband, Richard Bache; their family took good care of him. As he wrote to a friend, "I have seven promising grandchildren by my daughter who play with and amuse me, and she is a kind, attentive nurse to me."

Though he was not in the best of health, Franklin's mind was as brilliant as ever. He wrote many letters to friends all over the world. He described how he was busy planning additions for his house, including a new library for himself. He landscaped his yard, planting trees and shrubs. On long winter nights, he enjoyed cards and conversation with friends and family; and in the summer, he sat with them beneath a shady canopy of trees in the twilight and drank tea. He received visitors from all over, including his good friend, Thomas Jefferson, who came to give him news of Paris.

By 1787 America was in severe trouble. After the Revolutionary War the states began drifting apart from each other, for each behaved as if it were a separate country. There was no central government, no way to collect taxes, and no way to reach trade agreements.

In the spring of 1787 Franklin was chosen to be one of fifty-five delegates to attend the Constitutional Convention in Philadelphia. The convention's purpose was to plan one central government for the United States. Ben Franklin and his friend, George Washington, were the most famous delegates at the meeting. With Franklin's strong approval, Washington was chosen to be president of the convention. Soon Pennsylvanians were singing, "Great Washington shall rule the land, while Franklin's counsel guides his hand."

Although Ben Franklin was the oldest delegate at the convention, he never missed a session. His legs were so weak he had to be carried to and from the convention in a sedan chair. At Washington's suggestion the delegates always stood to greet him.

Franklin rarely spoke as the delegates spent four months designing the new government. But his very

An engraving of the Philadelphia State House, by W. Birch in 1778. (The Library Company of Philadelphia)

presence was an inspiration and helped calm tempers. At times he called for tolerance or prayer or told a funny story to relieve the tensions.

Even though Franklin had spent many years abroad, he was fiercely loyal to America. He was forever thinking about its identity as a new nation. He once wrote his daughter that he believed the turkey should be the national bird and not the bald eagle. He objected to the bald eagle because he said it stole food from the fishing hawk. The turkey was a better symbol because it was native to America and was useful, industrious, and courageous.

In the last year of his life Franklin took up his final cause—the fight against slavery. There was a time in history when few people questioned slavery. But gradually people of goodwill became repelled by the idea. When he was young, Franklin was not very concerned about the issue—his newspaper even advertised slaves for sale.

However by the time Franklin was eighty-four, he believed slavery was an outrage against humanity. He became president of the Pennsylvania Abolition

A Wedgwood cameo, depicting a slave, sent to Franklin when he was the President of the Pennsylvania Abolition Society. (American Philosophical Society)

Society. Arguing that all people are created by the same God and deserve equal care, he signed a paper, asking Congress to put an end to slavery. He also pointed out that freedom for slaves was an empty honor if they couldn't have education and economic power.

Ben's stand against slavery was his last public act. On April 17, 1790, when he was eighty-four years old, he died after a short illness. His favorite grandsons, Temple and Benny, were by his bed, along with his daughter Sally and her husband, and his British "daughter," Polly Stevenson.

In his will he left his library and all his manuscripts and papers to Temple. Unfortunately, Temple was so irresponsible that it was years before the papers were put in order; and by then many precious documents were lost. In his will Franklin also left a thousand pounds to both Boston and Philadelphia as a fund for young tradesmen who had been apprentices. And he left his favorite walking stick to his friend "and the friend of mankind, General Washington."

When Benjamin Franklin died, the House of Representatives wore mourning clothes for a month, as did the National Assembly of France. As one Frenchman wrote, "A man is dead, and two worlds mourn."

Twenty thousand people attended Franklin's funeral. It was the largest funeral ever held in Phila-

Print published in France announcing Franklin's death. (Given by Mrs. John D. Rockefeller)

delphia. Bells tolled throughout the city, and flags were flown at half-mast in the harbor. Perhaps his loved ones comforted themselves with words he'd once written when his favorite brother had died: "A man is not completely born until he is dead; why then should we grieve that a new child is born among the immortals?"

Ben Franklin does indeed seem to be immortal. In his lifetime he accomplished enough for more than a dozen lives: printer, writer, publisher, merchant, inventor, scientist, educator, colonial agent, politician, statesman, militia colonel, postmaster general, diplomat, and peacemaker. Though he "came up the hard way," the son of a candle maker moved through the worlds of America, England, and France with brilliance and humor.

The Encyclopedia Britannica once said about Benjamin Franklin: "A summary of so versatile a genius is impossible." But perhaps the best way to get the full impact of his remarkable existence is to read a list of his accomplishments:

Ben Franklin was one of America's first songwriters.

He was perhaps the best swimmer in the American colonies and a well-known swimming teacher in England.

He edited the best and the most successful newspaper in the Colonies.

He drew the first American newspaper cartoon and was the first to publish questions and answers in a newspaper.

He helped establish eighteen paper mills in the Colonies.

He established the first American newspaper printed in a foreign language.

He devised a reformed alphabet based on phonetic spelling.

He invented a copying press for making copies of letters and other writing.

He constantly wrote pamphlets, newspaper articles, and letters to promote the interest of his city, country, or the good of humankind.

He was author of the best-selling reading matter in the American colonies after the Bible: *Poor Richard's Almanack*.

He revised the Prayer Book of the Church of England.

He was responsible for the paving of the streets of Philadelphia.

He invented a better streetlamp for the city.

He organized the first street cleaning.

He established a police force.

He established a company of firemen.

He helped establish the first fire insurance company in America.

He helped fund the first hospital in America.

He organized the Junto club, the forerunner of the Rotary, Kiwanis, Lions, and Civitan clubs of today.

He was the founder of the American Philosophical Society.

He was the first American economist, the first president of the Society for Political Inquiries of Philadelphia—the first society in the United States that promoted the study of political economy.

He established the first successful circulating library.

He founded the University of Pennsylvania.

He was the first writer on education to recommend the teaching of modern languages.

He organized the first postal service and was the first postmaster general.

He was the first president of the Pennsylvania Abolition Society, advocating an end to slavery.

He discovered that lightning is electricity.

He invented the lightning rod.

He discovered that a current of electricity has a magnetic effect. (This is the principle on which the telegraph, telephone, and the electric motor are based.)

He demonstrated cooling by evaporation.

He advocated proper air ventilation.

He advocated building ships with watertight compartments.

He was the first to chart the Gulf Stream.

He was the first to discover that storms travel in the opposite direction from winds.

He is recognized as the father of the United States Weather Bureau.

He invented bifocals.

He invented a three-wheel clock.

He invented the Franklin stove, the first successful wood-burning stove.

He discovered a way to eliminate smoky chimneys.

He invented a library chair.

He invented an artificial arm for taking books down from high shelves.

He invented a one-arm chair to be used like a desk.

He invented the armonica.

He introduced the following plants and grains into America from Europe: Scotch kale, the kohlrabi, Chinese rhubarb, Swiss barley.

He promoted the cultivation of silk worms to make silk in Pennsylvania.

He introduced the yellow willow into America for basket weaving.

He introduced broomcorn into Pennsylvania from Virginia.

He introduced fowl meadow grass into England from America and the Newton Pippin apple.

He introduced Newton Pippin apples, and various American trees, nut-bearing trees, and shrubs into France.

He was the first to suggest the insurance of crops against storms, plant diseases, and insect pests.

He was the first to propose daylight saving time.

During the French and Indian War, he organized and commanded a regiment of 560 men to defend the Pennsylvania frontier.

At the opening of the Revolutionary War he planned the defenses of the Delaware River.

He devised a scheme for uniting the Colonies more than twenty years before the Revolution.

More than any other man, he was instrumental in securing the repeal of the Stamp Act.

In England and France he was the leading propagandist for the American Colonies.

He helped Thomas Jefferson write the Declaration of Independence.

He was our greatest diplomat, secured aid and millions of dollars for the Revolution from France. Without this our independence most probably would not have been won.

He was president of Pennsylvania for three consecutive terms.

He was the only one of the Founding Fathers to sign all five of the great state papers that achieved our independence: the Declaration of Independence, the Treaty of Amity and Commerce with France, the Treaty of Alliance with France, the Treaty of Peace with England, and the Constitution of the United States.

TIMELINE OF BENJAMIN FRANKLIN'S LIFE

1706	Born in Boston on January 17
1718	Became an apprentice to printer brother, James
1721	Became publisher of the *New England Courant*
1729	Published *The Pennsylvania Gazette*
1730	Married Deborah Reed of Philadelphia Appointed Public Printer by the Pennsylvania Assembly
1731	Established the first circulating library in North America
1732	Began the publication of *Poor Richard's Almanack*
1736	Organized the first fire company in Philadelphia
1737	Appointed postmaster of Philadelphia
1742	Invented the Franklin stove
1743	Began his experiments in electricity

1744	Founded the American Philosophical Society
1750	Elected to the Assembly of Pennsylvania
1752	Made his famous kite experiment and discharged electricity from the clouds
1753	Appointed deputy postmaster general of North America
1755	Supplied General Braddock's army in French and Indian War
1756	Introduced street paving, cleaning, and lighting into Philadelphia
1757	Went to England as agent of the Pennsylvania Assembly
1759	Given the title "Dr. Franklin" by the University of St. Andrews, Scotland
1766	Underwent examination in the House of Commons concerning repeal of the Stamp Act
1774	Dismissed by the British Government from office of deputy postmaster general in North America His wife, Deborah Franklin, died
1775	Returned to Philadelphia Elected delegate to the second Continental Congress Elected postmaster general of the Colonies

1776 Helped draft the Declaration of Independence
Appointed one of three Commissions to the Court of France, seeking aid for colonies

1778 Negotiated a treaty of alliance with France

1783 Negotiated a peace treaty with Great Britain, in which the independence of the United States was recognized

1785 Returned to Philadelphia
Chosen President (Governor) of Pennsylvania

1787 Elected delegate to the Constitutional Convention to help frame the Constitution of the United States

1789 Became president of the first society for the abolition of slavery

1790 Died in Philadelphia, April 17

BIBLIOGRAPHY

The Age of Revolution. New York: Golden Press, 1966.

CRANE, VERNER W. *Benjamin Franklin and a Rising People*. Boston: Little, Brown and Company, 1954.

FAY, BERNARD. *Franklin, the Apostle of Modern Times*. Boston: Little, Brown and Company, 1929.

FLEMING, THOMAS. *The Man Who Dared the Lightning*. New York: William Morrow and Company, 1971.

———, ed. *Benjamin Franklin: A Biography in His Own Words*. New York: Harper and Row, 1972.

FRANKLIN, BENJAMIN. *The Autobiography of Benjamin Franklin*. New York: Modern Library, 1944.

FREEMAN, DAVID. *Franklin*. New York: Harper and Row, 1976.

LOPEZ, CLAUDE-ANNE, AND EUGENIA HERBERT. *The Private Franklin*. New York: W. W. Norton & Company, 1975.

MILLER, JOHN C. *The First Frontier: Life in Colonial America*. New York: Dell Publishing Company, 1966.

MORAN, JAMES. *Printing Presses.* Berkeley, Calif.: University of California Press, 1973.

STEPHENS, BRAD. "Franklin's Outstanding Achievement," *The Amazing Benjamin Franklin.* Frederick A. Stokes Company, 1929.

VAN DOREN, CARL. *Benjamin Franklin.* Garden City, N.Y.: Garden City Publishing Company, 1941.

WRIGHT, ESMOND. *Franklin of Philadelphia.* Cambridge, Mass.: Harvard University Press, Belknap Press, 1986.

INDEX

ABOUT THE AUTHOR

Mary Pope Osborne has published four previous novels for young adults with Dial: *Run, Run, As Fast As You Can; Best Wishes, Joe Brady; Love Always, Blue;* and *Last One Home*. Of *Last One Home, School Library Journal* wrote, "Finely crafted characterization enhances this affecting story." Ms. Osborne brings her novelist's skill in characterization to this biography, her first nonfiction work for Dial.

Ms. Osborne grew up on Army posts throughout the country, mostly in the South. She divides her time between New York City and Bucks County, Pennsylvania, with her husband Will, and her dog Bailey. She is currently working on a biography of George Washington for young readers.